FONTAINE

Copyright (C) 2026 By Linda Carroll Barnes

Published By Linda Carroll Barnes

Photography by John Majure

All rights reserved. No part of this book may be reproduced, stored in a retrieval system or transmitted in any form or by any means — electronic, mechanical, photocopy, recording, or otherwise — without the prior permission of the author, except for the inclusion of brief quotations in a review and as permitted by U.S. copyright law.

This is a work of fiction. References to real people, organizations and events are meant to provide authenticity. Any resemblance to persons or names (other than historical events) is not intended.

Cover and interior design : Clyde Adams, ClydeAdamsBooks.com

ISBN Paperback : 979-8-9871955-2-9
ISBN Hardcover : 979-8-9871955-3-6

FONTAINE

A Southern Portrait of 1968

By Linda Carroll Barnes

CONTENTS

Dedication viii
The Descent 3
The Arrival 12
Together But Not Together 26
Meanwhile Next Door 34
Behold, A Pale Spring 47
"Our Town" 68
The Empire Of The Living 79
Just Peachy 93
Our Dreams Are Never Small 103
A Biscuit Buttered On Both Sides 114
Those With Power Over Us 125
The Hardware Man 136
We The Living 151
Gifts Of Yesterday 162
A Universe Afire 175
Does Heaven Reach This Far 188

DEDICATION

For all who served in Vietnam,
and for the ones who waited.

WINTER

Death would no longer be a distant stranger,
a thing that happened to other people.
It would happen to some of us.

CHAPTER ONE

THE DESCENT

Dawn melted over the edges of the world and found me here in the twilight of its first beginnings, my sleep washed in Eden's gossamer dreams, dewy deceptions willfully conjured to occupy a darkness at war with tomorrow. Dissolving the pale illusions of my escape, the insensitive glow slowly began devouring the earth, bathing me in its gauzy boundaries like a milky sky after a storm. I felt it then, the small exhilaration of accomplishment over the plain light fixture that hung now in the ceiling above our bed. Whit and I bought it together one morning, and we both laughed, ignoring its limited qualities and believing that its soft, round glow suggested images of constellations and candlelight. Like other young lovers, we expected too much. We went into town, pursuing domestic bliss among the cluttered bins and wooden floors of Donaldson's Hardware and Feed Store. Buoyed by the collection of all our new possessions; light fixtures and furniture, silver, crystal and fine china, it seemed to us that the universe had lately nodded approval to our recent arrival in the ranks of the young and married, and chose to spread this world's treasures before us.

Two years ago, it seemed like a lifetime now, Whit and I came home to the farm, to parties and large boxes delivered wrapped in heavy white paper tied with wide pink satin ribbon, full of silver platters and crystal goblets and toasters. How pleasant it was to unwrap them all and think of them as ours now, the accessories of our own fireside. There was a pleasing early morning heaviness to homemade quilts over the warm sheets of our double bed that begged an indefinite citizenship there. Nothing else breathed outside of those soft floral fragments sewn together by loving, aged hands and the faint perimeters of the blue ceiling above the faded walls, as if all of creation's moments were contained in this moment. The bed felt roomy as I opened my eyes now, in the way that beds do when a person sleeps alone and dawn thrusts out its first assault against the night, scouting the reluctant edges of curtains trailing at long windows. My mind slowly came to itself then, and I remembered. I recalled the thing kept only at bay by the numbing anesthetic of sleep, the thing I wanted so desperately to forget. I was alone here now.

The other side of the bed, the place where he would have been, was empty and cold, and nothing could change that. Whit was gone and he would be gone for a very long time. Or, maybe he was, like so many others, never coming back at all, never coming home. I would never see him vibrant and alive again in this life, burying him among his people, his headstone set in the dark earth of Fernwood beneath the aged spreading limbs and creeping azaleas rampant in a pink spring among old roses and wild violets. The descent into the sameness of it, that struggle every morning to survive without him another day, attached itself indelibly to my being now like an alternate apparition. I remembered the pain of the last good-by. I relived it again and again, tracing the shape of his face with my fingers, his gray eyes soft and resolute all at the same time, us both drowning in the moment, and holding on and on and on until we finally tore ourselves apart from the warmth of my hand in his.

Dressed in his travel khaki's, wearing a severe military haircut and his new wings, he and I drove up to catch the plane in Memphis, the city where he had been born. We walked out together onto the bright tarmac, watching the others in line ahead slowly make their way up the long stairs into the aircraft and turning to wave before disappearing inside. He bent to kiss me goodbye and whispered the things men say when they think it might be the last. We were brave, as other couples were in other wars, who said good-by to each other as we were doing now. We needed our courage to match the ordeal in front of us, and I didn't want a desperate face wet with tears to be his last glimpse of me. He had his own battles to fight now. But, as he left Fontaine, pulling out of his mothers front drive, she completely fell apart in the doorway, with a handful of tissues, crying her eyes out.

When a soldier goes away, separate futures are instantly created, paths that each person then walks alone. The family, the ones left behind, enter an unnerving no-mans land, gripped now in a steely and unfamiliar territory stretched wide in a yawning gap between hope and despair. It was 1968 and my young husband, like a host of other boys, was gone from us, from the safety and insulation of families and towns and schools and churches. He was in harms way, flying helicopters now in the skies over Vietnam, the hostile target of a treacherous enemy who inflicted immediate death, that permanent thing where a coffin arrives on an airplane and a family arranges a funeral now for an only son who died at twenty-one far away, in a foreign country among strangers.

Immediately I became a girl who only prayed one prayer, breathed it a dozen times a day.

— Please God, let him come home.

We and our contemporaries were not yet men and women but were in all essential ways still boys and girls, the carefree and the careless who just yesterday were in college, that diaphanous pre-school for life, the world of frat parties and unbridled romance, where chemistry tests and research papers were the zenith of our struggles. The war gave us, among other things, a crash course in growing up. It gave families; mothers, fathers, sisters, brothers, grandparents, cousins, uncle and aunts a new and unsettling common thread that bound them together now, cheerless and unrelenting. The old ways, the common greetings among them, were no longer used. Conversations didn't begin with innocuous discussions about the weather or personal well being or Friday night football. It was always the same, those first words…

— Have you heard from Whit?

There was no escape from it, and navigating this daunting new landscape became each day's challenge for us all. Some days we did well. On others, not so well.

How exactly had we arrived at this moment ? How did we get here, all of us living so close to the terrifying edge of a precipice, our lives and hopes bound to the one thing that joined us. If Whit wasn't in Vietnam, how different all of our lives would be. But, he was there, in that place, caught in the hostile events of the world we lived in, ruthless realities that thrust themselves upon us as they had in all prior generations. This formidable and daunting rearrangement of life was here now, just as surely as its previous claims on American history. We were a nation at war. At least some of us were at war. Many young men like Whit answered their countries call to go and fight the communists bent on the conquest of another country in Southeast Asia, Vietnam. The boys who could, avoided being drafted by getting deferments or joining a National Guard unit. Others found self expression by burning Draft Cards, marching in war protests and sometimes blowing up buildings, which seemed very extreme to me.

Proximity sometimes was everything, and we lived in the predictable cradle of the South where protesting anything was unknown and certainly frowned upon. The Evening News was our window to the world and every night we sat in Peach's living room in front of the television, a large square box with a screen width of about twenty inches, watching war footage and listening to a TV reporter read today's news from Vietnam; the battles, casualties, the enemy advancement and our generals' assessments of how the war was going. This was our only information about the far away place on the other side of the world where our soldiers, our boys, were fighting and dying. And, the boy we loved, this boy who was our whole world was there in that place, and that was all we cared about.

The hole in the fabric of a family, of a life, when someone leaves is no small thing. Everything is forever measured by memories of past times together; birthdays and ball games, afternoons down in the swimming hole, picnics at the lake and Sunday afternoons on the front porch. Sentences frequently begin with simple words that tell so much.

—Remember the time…we all went up the river and the boat sank…or that summer when Princess had nine puppies…or how Aunt Dotty always gave him a plaid shirt at Christmas?

These moments do not appear on the nightly news. No one sees a whole lifetime of caring and sacrifice except the people living it. And, when the wife of a fallen soldier is handed the folded flag from his casket, "On behalf of a grateful nation," it is a nice gesture, but not nearly enough. There is no replacement for the man who never walks through his front door again, never pitches baseballs with his boys, never helps his father change a tire, never teaches his daughter to ride a bike and never again does the thousand small things that we remember and cling to when he is gone.

At times, without permission, my night took on a life of its own; the unsettled, irregular patterns of the semi-conscious, immersed in vagrant dreams of jungles on fire and men screaming. I saw indistinct faces sometimes, men that I remembered well from flight school, so grand and handsome in their dress blues, drifting in a blue sea of military brass in a cavernous ballroom, all permanently bound together now by a pilot's uncertain aerial world of courage and tragedy. It was easy, in the sparkling atmosphere of this ornamented night, to remember the famous words from literature that stirred the hearts of the outnumbered troops at Agincourt, "We few, we happy few, we band of brothers, for he today that sheds his blood with me shall be my brother." Some of the men sitting here, affable and buoyant, drinking champagne at the white linen draped tables, framed against the blush of candlelight and flowers, were destined to join the fraternity of the fallen. They would leave this earth to live on only in the memories of wives and children, rising with their brothers, standing strong and resolute together among the ranks of the invisible somewhere in the beyond. In the night glow of the ballroom we smiled the smiles of the invincible and toasted the future of honorable men, a future with death and glory in it, and watched the resplendent images gliding among the slow, anonymous rhythms, pastel gowns and determined faces of their women. We were so young, glittering with courage and confidence, as if this night and all the nights would last forever. But, beyond the ballroom's illusions and decorum, another volatile world of irreverent terrors and nights of lethal sameness waited for me and for the others. There was no escape for any of us. The men we loved said goodbye, boarded the planes that took them away from us, from this luminous night into the deadly unknown, and we felt the finality of it settle in around us, the weight of our own war that was just beginning.

I slept at times with foreign images of infernos ablaze with the sounds and shapes of men, their twisted bodies staggering in the savage smoke of some battle, wrapped in the familiar deafening throb of our helicopters as they came around hard into an LZ (Landing Zone). The soldiers on the ground heard it, that early, faint sound, and looked up, scanning the sky, and straining to see those first dark shapes with rotating blades that lifted them out of their current hell. They ran hard toward the sound of the choppers and I saw them in the fight of their lives, their faces filled with despair and courage, the way heroes really look, covered in the mud of a thousand rice fields and someone else's blood. Sometimes through the mist, I caught the faint outline of a face like Whit's sitting in the cockpit of the helicopter rolling in through the hail of bullets to pick up those men, our men. Some of them would die, but not today. The pilots would turn back to base, unload, and go back again and again until darkness overtook them. I was overtaken myself, not by the inevitable arrival of earths coming night and another unquenchable morning, but by a kind of ruthless ferocity that attached itself to my dreams and waking hours alike, clinging to me like a semi-permanent garment.

More prayers may rise in the lonely carnage of battlefields than in churches, more desperate ones anyway. I remembered our Fly-By's at Fort Wyles; dozens of helicopters in the air together, crowding the sky in formation, the invariable sound announcing their approach. Graduation from flight school always ended with a Fly-By as each graduating class took to the air together for one last time. It was something to see. On post, I rushed outside, like every wife, eager to be there in that moment, to see the end of all the fierce hours of work every new pilot had endured through flight school. We wives had been there for it all, and now we wanted to be here at the end, our hearts full, watching them fly away into the bright days of promise. Prayers for their survival began that day. Before that, we prayed merely for their safety, but now the reality we had all so carefully evaded was upon us. Death would no longer be a distant stranger, a thing that happened to other people. It would happen to some of us.

Elsewhere on the planet (although it seemed to us like it really was occurring on another planet) war exploded on another front, a cultural divide now violently separating the present from the past. Youthful forces blew in on the drug fueled winds of change, arriving with the same intensity of a war, and became the new faces of the aggressive counter culture, the "Beat Generation" high on LSD, who opposed the war in Vietnam and just about everything else. I followed its progress with everyone here in the small world of our southern town, and wondered what to make of it all. Mere months ago in San Francisco some 100,000 hippies gathered in the communal scene of Haight-Ashbury to indulge in the freeing atmosphere of drugs, sex and psychedelic music, calling it, "The Summer of Love." It stuck, and now in the early days of 1968, they were all still replaying the memories of the Monterrey Pop Festival that drew over 200,000 warm young bodies wearing tie-dye, bell-bottoms and flowers in their hair. The "Flower Children" were known for their passion for non-violence and their commitment to being uncommitted, living sometimes in flower painted Volkswagen buses and sleeping under the stars in the warm, wild flower fields of California. Their message of "peace, not war" appeared everywhere; on clothing and jewelry and on graffiti painted city walls that were a new defining aspect of urban culture. Their more militant counterparts became the anti-war student marchers protesting in the streets of Berkley and Ann Arbor, carrying signs and dodging police tear gas. Whatever forms these new clashes with culture took, it was a movement that was obviously here to stay. But, like other families with soldiers in Vietnam, we cared about only one thing; the lives of our boys fighting and dying far away. We had little sympathy for the fluid, drug filled and sometimes violent characteristics of the "Beat Generation" counterculture. It would never attract us on this day or on any day.

CHAPTER TWO

THE ARRIVAL

An expected and inevitable winter arrived in north Mississippi, shrouding us all in a damp cold and the sheer grayness of it. And, unexpected by our forces, early on the morning of January 30, the Tet Offensive arrived in Vietnam when 67,000 Viet Cong and North Vietnamese attacked major and minor cities including Da Nang and Saigon. Khe Sahn was under siege and would continue to be for the next six months, until early July. In Huê, the formerly glittering provincial capitol, Marines and ARVN (Army of the Republic of Viet Nam) were the vanguard of ferocious fighting house to house that left the city in ruins. We saw the pictures of the carnage on the evening news and listened to our Commanding General say again with calm assurance that, "We could see the light at the end of the tunnel." But, now we were suspicious of the pronouncements of Generals and politicians, and we had generally stopped believing that there was any tunnel, or light at the end of it.

Exactly ten days before, on January 20, while the V. C. (Viet Cong) were preparing for the most memorable offensive of the war, our family launched its own personal counter measure and we didn't need 67,000 troops to do it. The event fundamentally and permanently changed life for us all, the impact reaching beyond our small town, spreading to family and friends in other towns and other states and eventually to Southeast Asia and the military base at Bien Hoa. I had our first child, born to us while her father was far away into a family yearning for some good news. I named her Isabel Mallory for my maternal ancestor, a woman made of serious material, but the family all called her Doll Baby. She was a major hit with eyes like mine that were brown and green all at the same time, and dark hair. She was going to be a beauty, dazzling and incandescent in her perfect pinkness. I tried not to ever picture her as fatherless, but in my mind I made myself see Whit standing there holding her all beaming and proud. He would be a great father and we would be an actual family in a white house with a picket fence and swings under an oak tree. She and I were our own little microcosm of a family, at least for now, and I wanted us to soldier on through everyday matching the same courage that Whit had. We would be brave and strong and he would be proud of us, but mostly he would be unburdened by letters from a complaining wife unable to cope with her hardships.

 I made a decision from the beginning that, whatever happened, Isabel and I would never wear the disheartening mantle of victims. Whit wouldn't have wanted that for us. Some wives lived in military towns and had each other for support. This wasn't their husbands first deployment. They had been separated before and knew the drill. But, since I was expecting our child, Whit wanted me to be in a safe place surrounded by family. My own parents were both still reeling from the misery and uncomfortable stages of the recently divorced, and in all my years of growing up, family tranquility and its natural companions of affection and contentment, never seemed to find us. So, I came here, a city girl, to this small Southern town into the arms of these caring strangers who would be my family now. My child would know them and they would love us both and somehow we would all survive these connected moments of a year that bound us all tightly together. There were no cell phones, no phone calls or computers or communications with a soldier halfway around the world. We were trapped daily in the vague and borderless land of not knowing. So, we all wrote letters to each other and the letters became everything. We filled our pages like diaries with details about the weather and spreading blackberry jam on our toast at breakfast or putting out purple pansies in the flower beds by our front porch. Even the smell of baby shampoo in Isabel's hair or how she reached for the butterflies suspended over her baby bed were small glimpses of home. Whit needed those, and our words to each other were a lifeline between us.

Those daily steps from the house out to the mailbox became a kind of pilgrimage, and I was a hopeful supplicant faithfully seeking the intervention of the Divine. Would there be a letter today? That moment became largely what I lived for. My pulse did beat a little faster. There was a tightness in my chest, almost holding my breath, the palpable tension of waiting, all by-products of wanting, of hoping. Emotions on the way to a mailbox…How could they exert such fierce intensity? The postman was not consistent in his rounds to our house, so reaching into the box became a little like Russian roulette. Would there be a letter or would there not be a letter? Had he come yet? When a trip to the mailbox elicits this kind of power over you, it tells you a lot about your life. Over time I developed the survival technique of infinite patience. I was supremely lucky

in regard to letters because Whit wrote me every single day and numbered them. The mail service from Southeast Asia being what it was, I sometimes missed a day or two, but then the numbered letters would arrive two or three at a time. So, Whit's daily letters became a thing I could count on, almost. Letters from husbands or boyfriends came much less frequently for other wives or girlfriends I knew. One friend in town, Sherry, always asked me the same routine question when we talked.

— Did you get a letter today?

Then she sighed knowing pretty much what the answer was. Her letters came about every other week, but her husband was out in a jungle somewhere near Cu Chi. At least that was the plausible explanation. The real truth was that he wasn't much of a letter writer and tired rather quickly of commitment to things he found uninteresting. Later on, that became obvious when he tired of her too, and found their relationship tedious and confining. He wanted another life and it didn't include her. Does the war change men? It certainly can, but sometimes the two personalities involved are simply crushed under the weight of circumstances that are larger than themselves. When this happened, the shattered pieces of a life had to be gathered up somehow and restored to a new normal that was already stained with grief over what had been irretrievably lost. Families had a lot of heavy lifting to do when a marriage disintegrated. Their suffering son or daughter needed help figuring out what life could look like now. Sherry's husband, who miraculously survived firefights in the thick, steaming jungles, came home from Vietnam and almost immediately left her in his new pickup for a new more appealing life in Nashville. Her family was distraught, never expecting that this boy from Columbus, whom they all loved and prayed for daily, would return to them a stranger anxious to find a new life without any of them in it.

Whit flew missions out of Bien Hoa, and at the end of every very long day, he sat down in the small room he shared with his roommate, Captain Riley, in their makeshift barracks and wrote to me about where the Assault Helicopter Company flew that day. I learned more about battles and combat and casualties from his letters than I ever did from the evening news. Pilots from his outfit and others were frequently wounded or killed. One close friend, Warrant Officer Raleigh Mitchell, had his leg nearly blown off on an early morning flight, filling the cockpit and the chin bubble of the aircraft with his blood. The crew chief tried desperately to tie off the arteries while the door gunner returned fire with his M-60's into a hot LZ (Landing Zone). Raleigh survived, but the Field Hospital sent him back to the states to recover. Late one afternoon, coming back from a flight delivering mail in the mountains, Whit took small arms fire from a tree line that caused a hydraulic failure and he autorotated down into a mine field. Somehow he and his crew managed to walk out.

On another day, I got the sad news that my good friend, Deanna, lost her husband, Sam, who died instantly when his helicopter went down in the South China Sea on a mission out of Da Nang. He had been in country for thirty-seven days. What would her life be like now? Words of comfort were hard when part of you was thanking God this wasn't your husband and your own stricken face watching him come home in a nondescript box. Or maybe he had been captured, or sometimes there was no box, no body, no closure, nothing to bury or mourn, just a semi-permanent state of grief. She crumbled beneath the enormous weight of it and a future she was unprepared for. When she called me from New York she could barely speak, and in the long months after, she struggled to find her own reason to live. She never found it really, and moved back in with her parents. Finally, she decided to go to nursing school which was a good start, but losing Sam left a permanent hole in her life that would never be filled. The lingering effect of losing someone you actually knew, whose wife you knew, was a silent grief that never quite went away because, down deep inside, you thought maybe tomorrow, maybe next week, it could be me. I desperately hoped that I never had to look into the sweet face of our own child, Isabel, and tell her that her daddy died in the Vietnam war in 1968.

Rebellion, that nimble and volatile occupation of the young was in full force from the very first seconds of 1968 staking claim to places like San Francisco, Chicago, Berkley, New York, Cambridge and Boston. Newly minted OFN (Our Freedom Now) leaders went down and hung out in Cuba, made idols of the revolutionaries and passionately committed themselves to their newfound infatuation with communism. The well informed read *Armies of the Night* and the *Electric Kool-Aid Acid Test*. College students were bathing in *Stanyan Street and Other Sorrows* and *The Feminine Mystique* along with "Do Not Go Gentle Into That Good Night" and the *Naked Lunch*. And, the protégée of a famed Russian dissident, Vladimir Popov, became the darling of western academics. The left-wing headwinds blew in the first beginnings of a subversive faction of campus radicals who eventually became very busy advancing the militant agenda that left three of them dead among pre-made bombs and dynamite in their Greenwich Village apartment. Even the sympathies of American expatriate poets found their way into the literary spectacle, brought to us all the way from Italy.

America it seemed, was a seething cauldron of unrest. Students protested against the war, the government, capitalism, segregation, inequality, farm ownership, chemical companies and even beauty pageants. Nothing apparently, was safe from what appeared to be a disturbing cocktail of discontent, and we watched it all unfold on television. The advent of evening news with access to actual footage of the days events was a new thing, a technological marvel and we, like the rest of the nation, sat mesmerized every night. Whit's parents, Whitney and Cynthia were horrified. Whitney came home from WWII to a peaceful and grateful nation, and said he had never seen anything like this. Whit's grandmother, Peach, just sat there silently shaking her head from side to side.

These were students my age raging out there on the streets and peering through the windows of a hostile take-over of some campus building. They were my age, but they were not my people. My people were those sitting here diffidently in this room, our small, abbreviated sanctuary from the perpetual unrest. And there, night after night, I began to feel the first beginnings of resentment toward the marchers... abrasive, arrogant, unapologetically opposed to pretty much everything, especially the war that my own husband was fighting that day. My resentment continued to grow and become anger when I watched our soldiers, the lucky ones who made it back to the states, on the receiving end of vitriol or indifference. The anti-war protesters ferociously called them "baby killers," an unrelenting label that hung in the air everywhere. No returning soldier escaped it. Any gratitude for their service, for spilled blood and months of living with death came from the strongholds of family and friends in places where they were known and loved, not the world at large. The America that welcomed home its men from WWII with parades and celebrations apparently didn't exist anymore.

So, while these youthful protesters were bent on changing the world, daily upending the ground they occupied, we really couldn't afford to give them the power to affect ours. When the news was over and the last casualties of the day were read, one of us just got up and turned off the TV set. Then we talked about where the battle had been that day and if it had been close to Whit. His dad usually had something to say about the damned politicians running the war, but we tried to be optimistic. We needed to believe and keep on believing that the war was going well and maybe Whit would be home soon. Sometimes it was just me and Peach watching the news together in the house I shared with her, but it was always the same. One of us got up and turned off the TV and we just looked at each other for a long minute, unable to even process or comment on what we just saw. We developed an almost nightly ritual. We both went on into the kitchen where there was always a coconut or chocolate cake she kept in the ice box. In her house we called it the ice box, never the refrigerator. In her lifetime, before electricity came to kitchens, there was a tall vertical metal box with a door, shelves for food and a place for a large square block of ice that kept the interior cool until it melted and was replaced by another brand new block of ice. The blocks of ice came from the Ice House in town, and an ice box was, in its day, the pinnacle of a modern kitchen. We ate narrow slices of cold cake, just the two of us, and talked about sewing or the garden or whether it was warmer than usual for this time of year, and there was mundane safety in that, safety in the whole house that Whit's ancestors had built.

By now Peach had buried a husband, A. W., and two brothers, both parents, grandparents and assorted uncles and aunts. She was no stranger to death. More than one body had been laid out for a wake in the front room this house, but there was no mournfulness anywhere within these walls. The house felt solid and safe like the refuge, the home it had always been. It wasn't a grand place, just a sprawling country home with plenty of room for a large family and even the entire high school basketball team Whit's dad, Whitney, brought home after a game one night to all be fed, unannounced. When WWII came along they added an addition to the house, a one bedroom apartment to rent out to the new workers at the overflowing new ordinance installation out in the county. This addition, built to house strangers in a time of war, was my home now, and was again another harbor in another time of war. It connected to the main house by a door at the end of a long hallway. Though not large, it had everything Whit and I needed including a bath and small kitchen with a gas stove and windows looking out at thick oak and pecan trees. We came here right after we married, before he started flight school, and now I was back again in the apartment we painted pale yellow with Peach's homemade curtains on the windows.

Peach's white house with green shutters, built of hand-sawed local pine, sat at the end of a winding gravel road shaded by a pecan orchard laced with large oaks. We were miles from our town of Fontaine on 465 acres of family land south of Memphis that had been in the family since 1889. Peach and her late husband, A. W., farmed it together, raising cotton and dairy cattle like his father before him. The house reflected the setting and the people in it. A dark front door with oval glass opened from the long front porch into the parlor that we called a living room now. Wallpaper, carefully glued to feed sacks over rough sawn boards covered the walls of every room. Perfectly smooth, flat and done in varying shades of green, I wondered how long it must have taken to paper all those walls with ten foot ceilings. Good floors of old Mississippi pine stretched through all the rooms, worn in some places and aged by decades of Rutledge feet.

Arthur Whitney Rutledge, III was Whit's given name. His daddy was Whitney, and his granddaddy had been simply A. W. to everyone. They lost A. W. early to an accident on a neighboring farm when he was just forty-five. Whit was only three. Peach never re-married or even learned to drive, but had for years managed the house and this whole place of cotton and cows with the sometime help of her two boys and assorted hired help. Some of them lived on the place in a few of the make-shift houses hastily put up during the height of the war. These were all mostly gone now or used to store hay or feed. I really had no idea when I married Whit, of his deep attachment to this place. It grieved him to leave it, and our favorite times together were our evening walks down in the pasture just when the cows came up at dusk and the cool night air settled over the smell of damp fields.

I made my way down toward the fields alone now, along the uneven path through the ragged grass past the barn where the earth sloped away to acres of good bottom land back-lit by the fading mist of green and gold. The sky changed, the quiet deepened to the early mauve of evening, and I wondered how many others there were. How many other bone-tired men and women walked this place or farms just like this, stood together leaning on the fence rail counting cows or figuring how much it would cost to repair the roof of the barn and talking about whether it was too early to start the tomatoes. I saw the romance in it, the attachment to a place, the inescapable yearning to walk your own ground. Evening after evening I put on my boots and old plaid field coat and walked that same path, looked out at the same fading, purple whispers of night and leaned against that fence like Whit would do if he was here. I felt just the slightest suggestion of his presence then, as if the strength of his yearning reached all the way from the ground of Southeast Asia to the earthy, scented ground of cows in this lake field. As much as Whit wanted to return home to me, maybe way more, like young men of generations before him, he just wanted to come back to the holy ground of home. He wanted to come back to this.

He heard early that sound known to a class of men, the hunters horn, that binds them to the land and everything associated with it. His enthusiasm for this place rose in him like a spring, probably the same atavistic inclinations of his fathers, alive in him now and strong enough to last. I pictured him here always, in the soft glow, looking out toward his hunting woods, thinking the thoughts men think about the ground that claims them. There would be deer feeding down in the dense overgrowth that hugged the intermittent creek fed by the river when the rains came in the spring. The wild hogs that occasionally plagued us left trails among the pines and high thickets that fell away to our plowed fields, asleep now and at rest. Rabbits and raccoons took shelter among the fallen trees and hollowed logs as their ancestors had, roaming the same trails and drinking from the same rocky pools beneath the fallen amber leaves. Whit belonged here among them in the deep quiet of this forest, more than any other place on this earth.

CHAPTER THREE

TOGETHER BUT NOT TOGETHER

I never had it, this love for the land, but Peach did. She understood it, and like her near neighbor, Miss Alma, took her strength from it. Some recorders of history would later write that the peopled landscape of this rural, bucolic world never really existed, that it was entirely an American fiction of something that wasn't, couldn't have been real. But, it was intensely real to us, the ones actually living it. I think Miss Alma would have laughed out loud at the notion that her life wasn't "real." It sure felt real. She had buried three husbands. One fell out of a hayloft and broke his neck. Another caught the chill of a late spring helping a neighbor roof his house and died immediately from pneumonia. The last just passed quietly with a heart attack sitting on the front porch. If you wanted sympathy or a shoulder to cry on Miss Alma's was the wrong place to go. She just looked at you like you were as weak as water.

—Honey girl, you've just got to keep on keepin' on, she'd say. That was the extent of her philosophy about pretty much everything.

She seemed undaunted by adversity in general and managed along with everything else to excel at growing roses and making chess pies that she always entered in the County Fair. She raised a flock of fat white chickens, and Doll Baby and I bundled up and rode out there to her place sometimes to get eggs and homemade butter.

We sat in her warm parlor and talked about the weather for starters. That was a given, and then we talked about the condition of the roads and whether the city had repaired those bridges over the low places where the river came up. On the mantle over the fireplace was a picture in an old gilt frame of her younger brother Grady who died tragically in the mustard gas and trenches at Burgoyne, and beside it, tied with narrow black ribbon, were stems of dried roses from his casket. This was her only remembrance of him, but she never talked about it. I noticed that the women in her circle, the ones who came to make quilts and help her put up corn didn't say much, didn't do their grieving out loud. Their compassion was a silent thing for times when words weren't nearly enough. An understanding of death just hovered in the somber stillness of the room after some loss, and there wasn't the need to say a single thing.

I watched the ladies with their nimble fingers sometimes as they made the tiny stitches, sitting in their circle, the quilt top stretched out between them. Someone was getting married, and this was the gift, their gift of time and labor and sentiment. They didn't use the word love too much, but their affection for each other was clear and had been for decades. They were people who did not have to explain themselves to each other. Lucy's boy, Arliss, was engaged to Martha's girl, Luellen, something to be glad about, something to plan. There was a church to decorate, with cake in the church hall afterwards, and flowers to gather and dresses to make. I never saw women more adjusted to their circumstances. They rose to every occasion. They found a way through, a way to survive, and all without any assistance from anyone. They were unmoved by the prevailing winds of social change sweeping the country, changes like war protests and Women's Lib. Information was deposited in their living rooms by the Evening News, and our conversations sometimes touched on the animated scenes of bearded, unwashed young men and hostile young women. There seemed to be two concurrent sisterhoods, two separate riparian paradigms, one a raging torrent bent on change, the other, an antediluvian stream incrementally finding its way between the smooth stones through still and quiet pools. Clearly, I was drawn to their quiet perseverance. It had been saving them for decades.

Miss Alma always gave us a package or two of purple hull peas she put up from the summer and a free lecture on parenting because, obviously, I was too young to know anything about life or raising children. Though she never had children of her own, she had definite ideas about what to do with them. Severe in many of her ways, she was ridiculously soft when it came to babies. She bounced Isabel on her lap and told her what a pretty thing she was, that she was the prettiest baby there ever was in this world and wasn't her mama lucky to have such a precious thing. She went on and on, loving every minute of it, and I let her. Watching a baby be so loved was something to see. We finally tore ourselves away and Miss Alma went back to pitching hay or piecing a quilt or crocheting baby blankets or one of the thousand other things she knew how to do. Then, Doll Baby and I went home to cook up our purple hull peas for supper with Peach.

I did have other places to go…town, where Whitney and Cynthia lived in their gracious new home eleven and a half miles away. It was difficult to imagine two people more unsuited, and I marveled at their ability to tolerate each other. They lived together, but they were definitely not together. Cynthia was the woman men dream of and other women admire, a bright and shining star; educated, beautiful, stylish, articulate, and the sparkling hostess of luminous parties with champagne, cucumber sandwiches, tiny ham biscuits and Charlotte Russe served impeccably on heavy family silver. She played very aggressive Bridge, an early accomplishment acquired during her college sorority days. She knew everybody worth knowing in the surrounding counties, or maybe the entire state. In addition, most of all, and more importantly, she liked to shop more than any woman I ever met, a thing which bound us immediately to each other. I'd never had a mother-in-law, and Cynthia never had a daughter-in-law so we both were new at this. We both wanted to be friends, and in not very long at all, we were.

On occasion, we took the narrow Highway 78 north out of town, drove a little over an hour, shopped all day in Memphis and spent the night at the Peach Tree Hotel. We came home the next day, her large white sedan loaded with bags and boxes. Then Cynthia spent a week trying on everything she had brought home on approval, because trying on clothing in those hot store dressing rooms was too taxing and inconvenient. I was right there with her on that and my job was to grab anything off the racks that had potential and drag them in piles to the dressing room for her potential approval. We were ruthless, culling out unworthy dresses, shoes and hand bags to make room for another load. This was serious business, the serious business of shopping, and we had no time to waste. Other matrons of Memphis had the luxury of leisure, but not us. We needed to stay focused so that when we got up the next morning at the Peach Tree we had made a substantial dent in local Women's Ready to Wear and were ready for the run south to Cynthia's headquarters, her boudoir, that sacrosanct sanctuary for the end results of retail therapy. I loved her instincts and unerring eye for quality. She knew immediately what to keep and what to cull. She could have made a fortune as a buyer. It was exhausting. Eventually hunger forced us to stop for lunch at Bishop's Cafeteria or some place like that where we ate very quickly and got back to the real business at hand, shopping. I admired her focus and her fortitude. It was a crash course in Textile Merchandising.

Cynthia did have a few flaws, the most serious one being the fact that in spite of all her good looks, good qualities and good deeds, she had been raised to be spoiled and selfish and expected to have everything her way all of the time. It was obvious to me that Whitney, long ago, just gave in and gave up. He sat in his chair over by the fireplace intent on his newspaper with that grim look on his face. Then after a while, after whatever scene they'd had was over, some time went by and they did it all over again. My young mind suspected that Cynthia just needed and expected a bigger stage, and she yearned to live in grand style in Memphis, miles and miles away from their ties to the farm, married probably to a state senator, or at least the mayor. She escaped every now and then into the understanding arms of her family over in Corinth, who petted and cajoled her, sympathizing with her discontent of being married to a man like Whitney who obviously never understood or appreciated her. He had ambition, enough to rise as a corporate executive, enough to become chairman of the Hospital Board, spend Thursdays at the

Civitan Club and Wednesdays at the Fontaine Economic Council. He'd been the magnetic and cultivated president of his fraternity, probably one of the things that attracted Cynthia to him. Whatever he was or wasn't, Cynthia just lost sight of it pretty often until so much damage had been done that it was too late to fix.

Theirs wasn't the only relationship I knew about that functioned that way and I wondered if possibly I might be staring at my own future. Continuing Education for me wasn't in the classroom now, but among adults in the real world who struggled with their own imperfections and glaring failures. The war compounded it all and made it harder to stay steady. But, rising almost against our will, our primitive instincts, the desperation of survival bound us tightly to each other, too.

After a few days of recovering from the latest unpleasantness, when Cynthia had enough consolation, she came back home with her perfect hair and perfect clothes, ready to start again. She was my first glimpse of a fragmented and complicated personality unable to ever be in harmony with itself. I could have, and was tempted often, to feel hard toward some of her more unexplainable behavior, but in the end, the innate sympathies of women for other struggling women won out. I tended to think that the pressure of Whit's ever-present exposure to death was very hard on her. The blanket of fear, woven with its million threads of loss and grief and apprehension fell upon her from the first, tenaciously attaching itself, her senses brimming day and night with visions of her boy who might never come home again. She wasn't alone in that. They buried Margaret Allen's only child, John, at Fernwood on a Thursday morning, her standing there in black, bent with grief in the cold rain of winter. Already a widow, she was alone now, her face stricken to the core and there was no expression of consolation that seemed adequate. Cynthia hugged her and they exchanged a glance that said everything, and then Cynthia went home with the blanket of fear around her tighter than a second skin.

These occasional deaths of our young men appeared appropriately in the Obituary Column of our paper, The Sentinel, mostly next to some aged person who passed away from the usual inconvenience of just being old. They were seventy-nine, or sixty-three or fifty-seven. But, "John Allen passed away on February 12, 1968 at age 20," had an unsettling effect, almost demanding that it be read over and over for it to seem real. The newsprint in stark black felt cold, clinical and unsympathetic. It was the merely the dutiful announcement of today's news, today's deaths minus compassion, filling the long space beside the grocery ad of weekly specials from Adlers Grocery and the women's shoe sale at The Ideal shop. After that, when I saw Margaret Allen on the street or in a store she had that resolute look, the kind that Miss Alma had, a look without any softness in it. All the light was gone from her eyes now, and they were dull and dark from weeping. John's picture in a gilt frame sat on her mantel too, now, just like Miss Alma's. He had been so alive then, so alive and smiling at the kitchen table, joking about their shared affinity for bacon and biscuits and putting an arm around her shoulders as she bent over the stove. Those days were over, so completely over, but still sometimes, she told me, she kept expecting him to walk through the front door.

He lived confined to the current Now thrust upon us all, in that narrow and shadowy world of memory, a vintage sepia image in somber brown like all the other frames on all the other mantles, among studied soldier's faces, unlined and strong with hints of fortitude and determination. But there was in each face something more, in an indefinite expression or tilt of the head or squared posture, the unmistakable boyish apparition of youth, that lively and spirited enthusiasm and hopefulness found only in the young. Miss Margaret and Miss Alma and hundreds of other women just like them sat alone now late at night eating a cold leftover supper and thought of their boys and prayed for their souls and wondered how to make it through another night, and the next night and the next. Seeing her always made me hesitate, and reminded me, made me think that kindness is often the road best traveled, and we forgive people for a lot of things when they are really just doing the best they can.

CHAPTER FOUR

MEANWHILE NEXT DOOR

Peach and I had no close neighbors, the nearest being her other son, Whitney's younger brother, R. J. and his wife, Ilene. They lived not far down the old road to town with their two boys who were in High School. They were in and out of Peach's house all the time, eating cake or leftover fried chicken or cantaloupe slices out of a gallon jar in the ice box. R. J. had managed to make himself into a planter with over a thousand acres of good Mississippi bottom land under cultivation in our county and the one next door on the east edges of the Delta. He and Whitney couldn't have been more different, and their wives couldn't have been more different. Gregarious and congenial, R. J. managed to keep Ilene and the boys soothed and mostly contained, but it was like trying to herd cats. She was a book reading, liquor drinking, ecumenical type with academic friends and R. J. was more like a glorified "good ole boy" whose favorite subject was farm machinery. Like Whit's parents, they met at college and married immediately and unwisely. I wondered what caused this until I remembered that Whit and I had done the same thing. What prompted three Rutledge men to marry flashy city women who would look so unfavorably on life at the farm? I might have been sort of flashy but not in the same league with Cynthia and Ilene. I wondered what I would do if Whit decided to stay here on this place, and part of me just wanted to be with him wherever he was. Nearby Fontaine didn't seem all that bad. People here seemed mostly happy, mostly content, and I told myself maybe that was enough. Cynthia and Ilene found a way to survive. Maybe I could, too. Whether mere survival was enough was something I shut out of my mind. I loved Whit, and for now, that was all that mattered.

R. J. didn't appear to have any serious vices because Fontaine was a small town of around twenty-nine thousand and he was a dedicated church goer. The opportunities for sin were limited. It was like being on a reservation of sorts, and nobody ever left. It just wasn't done. Some ladies I came to know in town refused to even visit me way out there "across the river" and they asked the same question pretty much over and over.

— When are you going to move to town?

Occasionally, livestock wandered across the road out in the county, local herds used to roaming from field to field. The city ladies found this disturbing, and they were equally anxious about venturing as far as Memphis, terrified by the prospect of automobiles driven more than thirty-five miles an hour. R. J. took all the ruffled city ways with a grain of salt and was just happy counting his money and raising his boys to do exactly what he had done, hunt and fish and farm. Ilene invited her ecumenical friends to sit with her in her wicker chairs out under their oak trees sipping bourbon, eating toasted pecans and discussing literature, something that eventually came to benefit me. Essentially, because their property was a big place, she and R. J. didn't have to see each other all that much. She was, in all respects, a very cultivated woman who taught me right away the importance of two things; cooking and reading.

Her kitchen never felt the terrifying absence of simmering pots and pans. She believed that an empty stove made men nervous, and they were best managed with full and happy stomachs. Roasts simmered in thick brown gravy. Chili and beans seasoned with homemade deer sausage clung to the back burner. Fried chicken and catfish never disappeared and deep dish pie it seemed, was always in the oven. Her potato salad was famous, but she was legendary for her creamed onions, smothered in a delectable sauce that clung to each sliver like the Gold of Orpheus. Being around her was certainly stimulating, and she managed somehow to teach at the college and cook and read and entertain without succumbing to the usual forms of female anxiety. She had a low tolerance for inefficiency of any kind. Her home reflected a long history of collecting religious artifacts, sculpture, exotic fragments and art by people with unpronounceable names including fine reproductions of *Adoration of the Magi* and *The Birth of Venus*. A small stone she gathered from a narrow path on her pilgrimage to Rocamadour sat on top of a first edition of *All the Sad Young Men*. The environment was delicious, a perfect consommé of objects previously unknown to my still adolescent senses. She did have apparent vices that set her decidedly apart from the church ladies in town, except for the worshipers in the small, quaint cathedral on the corner who embraced her with the fervent charity of one of their own. She smoked like a chimney and drank like a sailor, but she did it with style. They were her people, and the non-denominational people were not, so R. J. went to the their citadel on the most prominent corner in town with the fat white columns and worshiped with one-hundred and fifty-eight others whom he had known since birth. He sat on the third pew to the left and sang "A Mighty Fortress Is Our God" on page 37 of the green hymnal, which he had done since he could squeak out his first notes, over a thousand times now in his forty odd years of sitting in exactly the same place.

R. J. talked about his religion with fervor. He often spoke of saving souls and reaching the lost. He took it seriously and insisted Doll Baby and I go to church with him, so we did. Sometimes tears formed in his big soft eyes when he talked about praying for Whit, for him to come home safe to us. We rode all over God's creation in his fancy silver Pick-up with air conditioning. Never have I seen a man so rooted to the soil and its history. He knew everything; how the river came up in '27 and washed away almost an entire block of town, leaving only one stone column from the post office. The Bourbon roses planted in the pristinely cultivated pocket garden by the riverside park came from the cuttings of Mrs. Dorothea Henderson of Natchez. In a flurry of good will, she had offered him her prized Zephirine Drouhin and the celestially white Souvenir de la Malmaison. One wonders how the details of the holy transfer might have been accomplished. Did he, as an emissary of the city, personally drive south to collect them ? He always uttered the name of Natchez with reverence and I wondered if he and Dorothea might have had some past history other than rose cuttings. He did manage to make business trips routinely that took him south to Vicksburg and beyond, driving the Trace down to Natchez. Dorothea apparently came from a cotton family up in the Delta and there was some common thread between them that went all the way back to a society party in Memphis. Did they have some kind of "understanding" between them? Did her family interfere, as was often the case, because R. J. was insufficiently wealthy at the time? Whoever she was, they enjoyed an enviable warmth that apparently survived for decades. He was a man who worshiped Southern womanhood, and the lovely and cultivated Dorothea apparently epitomized that. Why, her family had been in Washington County for decades before the "Wowa"...That's the way everybody here pronounced war, and they always meant The War, The War of Northern Aggression.

People here still talked about it as if it happened last week. And, everybody knew exactly where their ancestors had served, fought and died.

—My great-great uncle, Fortis Buchanan lies buried at Shiloh. He died a valiant death in the fighting in April, 1862. It still grieves us all to think of him laid to rest in Tennessee soil.

—Major Chapman, my momma's great grandfather, was killed tragically in an explosion aboard the steamboat Bella Rose near Helena. His body and twenty-three more were sadly never recovered.

I had R. J. to thank for an education not available in any college. My own people were not exactly landed gentry. They farmed good Southern soil in Arkansas and Alabama for decades, my Daddy's folks over in Florence along the winding artery of the Tennessee River. They finally moved away from the land, farther south to Gulfport and became city people. But, like all the Southerners I knew, they talked of The War and our ancestors place in it without any difficulty in remembering these events that occurred a mere hundred years ago. The pain of it had scarred them, scarred everyone who endured it and those who lived through the aftermath of Reconstruction. Nobody was going to forget that or that Sherman marched through Georgia and burned Atlanta.

The suffering of our people was palpable and perhaps one of the things that bound us all close. WWI, WWII and the current war in Vietnam were similar in that way; the specter of death hovered over us all. There was no adequately explaining it. It was a misery to be endured, without sufficient expressions or remedies, only understanding looks that said a thousand words. So, we shared those among ourselves and kept on everyday doing what our people had always done. We watched our boys pack their bags and leave the trophy lined shelves and floral wallpaper and sheer, tie-back curtains in the bedrooms of their youth, wave good-bye and get on trains or planes and leave us. Our women cried, our men looked on with grim understanding, and everybody prayed for their safe return. We were part of the same picture, just wearing the clothes of a different century.

After church, after R. J. and Isabel and I stood around talking for the appropriate length of time, which wasn't long because the church ladies all wanted to get home to get their roasts out of the oven, we pulled out of the church parking lot in the line of others in a hurry for their Sunday dinners and headed back to Peach's. Her usual Sunday offerings entirely filled up the ancient and now groaning table with predictable platters and bowls of mashed potatoes, gravy, fried chicken, butterbeans, squash, Ilene's creamed onions and Cynthia's pea salad. We used all the leaves for the table and all the chairs because all of us were there to be fed; Whitney and Cynthia, R. J. and Ilene and their boys, Isabel and me and sometimes visitors lucky enough to be invited. You could seat fourteen easily around that table and sometimes it was full. On the sideboard sat coconut cake, chocolate cake, buttermilk pie and cherry pie, or sometimes peach or blackberry that we picked down by the old fence near the bottoms. Peach always had four desserts. She believed we should all have our favorites and had the second slice already on a plate the very second the first slice was gone. If anybody declined a second piece because they were too full right then, her face would register disappointment. She felt deeply the importance of feeding us all and feeding us well. Usually we remembered that, took the second slice with the grateful look that warmed her heart and just took a while to eat it. Peach cooked as other people practiced their religion, with devotion, and we were all the supplicants, the consecrated beneficiaries of her sacred benevolence. Most of us succeeded in appropriate levels of gratefulness. The rowdy boys would only appreciate much later the benefits of having dined at her table, after she was gone, the faint images of the fried chicken and green wallpaper clinging fast to their memories with tenacious fingers that lingered on and on and on. They would remember then. And, Cynthia, certainly the least grateful person at our ceremonial dinners would have, at some point, only the history of her excellent pea salad, served cold, accompanied by her other side-dish, uncongenial indifference, also served cold.

Cynthia, Whit's mother, loathed these dinners, hated the farm and by the time dinner was over, had about exhausted her resources of good will. Unfailingly cordial, she quietly removed herself to the front porch to drink iced tea, recover from the strenuous requirements of polite conversation and chat with Ilene while the rest of us cleaned up and the men talked about football and ate pie and cake. Cynthia was, among her many other accomplishments, a fabulous cook who was just as famous for her squash casserole and spoon bread as Ilene was for her creamed onions and potato salad. Anyone who had ever tasted her spoon bread never forgot it. It was the most deletable arrangement of grits possible this side of heaven, and it even had the power to change an unpleasant person into a nice person with one single bite. One gentleman described it as "Manna of the Gods," when he struggled to find adequate praise.

I had dinner at Whitney and Cynthia's house for some luminary one night, a local person of consequence. He wore a grey suit and a grey tie and was, I think, a bank president or something. I wasn't sure his wife, Edith, cooked much because he came unescorted and Edith begged off with a headache. The truth was she didn't want to be upstaged by Cynthia's spoon bread. Well, the man, whoever he was, did, in hushed tones, pronounce it "Manna from heaven," and began quietly dissolving in the holy moment right there at the table. I think he came close to tears. The conversation softened and good will began its slow rise to the surface, revealing a sought after contentedness that eclipsed the serenity usually found in church. After three bites, we were already bathed in a sacred alliance of comradeship that rendered us helpless against the Bourbon soaked lady fingers of Charlotte Russe to come.

Edith was probably wise to avoid this kind of culinary rivalry. Nobody could compete with Cynthia's spoon bread, and memories of the evening's success would only bring ill will later on when her husband mentioned the Holy experience, probably at breakfast when she was not at her best. Nobody wanted that. The fallout from such elaborate dinners tended to last indefinitely, and the resentful wife was forced to put extravagant recipes in the Ladies Auxillary Cook Book just to save face. She might even allude to a chummy relationship with some foodie whose name glowed in the luminous lights of a trendy bistro. This was useful cover because it associated her with a pretentious food experience whether or not she actually cooked anything at all. She could always resort to name dropping and talk casually about her useful dining experiences at Chez Henri as if she and Henri himself were old and fast friends who vacationed together in the South of France and spent hours exploring les fromages et vins de Provence. The world of dinner guests in a small town could be a slippery slope, and quite a few dining invitations required careful management. One usual solution was to simply decline using some plausible excuse. That lifted the pressure of having to reciprocate and be forced to accomplish some unachievable level of even the most standard chicken and rice casserole. Some reluctance also reflected the hostesses unwillingness to entertain guests for other reasons. I heard more than one woman's hushed admission that she didn't want to have company because she would "have to clean the whole house." The complicated business of dinners and dinner parties seemed best left to those natural hostesses like Cynthia or Ilene who were equipped to turn out a superb soufflé and manage escargot without setting the table cloth on fire.

After our communal encounter that evening with Cynthia's spoon bread and ample glasses of an appropriate Bordeaux, Whitney adjourned the table, drawing our now impaired guest to his blue leather chairs in the den where he succumbed to a last helping of Charlotte Russe and a demitasse laced with enough Bourbon to satisfy all the distillers in Kentucky. They talked in subtle tones of gentlemen about the sorry state of politics and Bobcat football and who belonged on the River Commission. He was sufficiently numb and contented when he finally rose to leave. Cynthia and I each took an arm securing him firmly between us and walked him from the clubby comfort of Whitney's den to the front door, charming him with the usual comments women know that bank presidents like to hear. As he drove slowly away we felt pretty sure that any time any of us needed a loan, he was our man. The fact that Whit was risking death every day to defend the ideals of American freedom and democracy warmed him and he rose enthusiastically to our defense in a way customary to officials, civic leaders and clergymen. They all wanted to do anything they could for "our boys." I was buoyed, as I always was, by the warmth of support. What a nice man. One thing was for sure, he would never, ever turn down an invitation that included Cynthia's spoon bread.

SPRING

…if only his body came home to us, his last breaths expended on a battlefield, then he would lie here, safe in the same ground with his family… at Fernwood. The old pink roses, long planted here at the edge of the plot, waited for him…

CHAPTER FIVE

BEHOLD, A PALE SPRING

Airport, the latest taut drama unfolded on the pages of my paperback book. The beach was warm underneath my limp body and the sand crept covertly between my toes and into the creases behind my knees. In the brand new novel, two lovers, both victims of loveless marriages offered each other sympathy and comfort in the icy grip of the frozen runways of a fictitious Chicago airport. An unfolding tragedy prepared to engulf them all, blizzards and bombs and domestic discord, the thrilling stuff of fiction. While I digested this, I toasted my white body and Isabel napped on the perfect beachfront of the Bay Water Resort in Biloxi, Mississippi.

Spring had come early to us in Fontaine and with it the early first daffodils and forsythia, then primroses and azaleas, eager to free themselves from the cold earth. Our flower beds at the farm were dotted with lavender hyacinths in an amethyst madness beneath the redbuds and dogwoods, the staggering drifts of crenelated snow drops valiantly rising among the dark leaves of winter. There would be iris's later and wild honeysuckle, and then the hydrangeas tucked among the laurels would come into their own, daring the snowballs to surpass their voluminous announcement of an impending summer. The pine boughs, heavy with all the years of green, reached down with outward arms toward the earth mingled with the twisted oaks until our paradise was secure, impenetrable by anything that did not belong here in our Arcadia. How I came to rely on the leafy associations, the gatherings of blossoms in their innocent liaisons with feathery ferns and vagrant lilies. Nothing could touch it, and there was comfort in that.

There was even comfort in the wide, uneven front walk that had once been solid brick. But, now the earth was busily claiming them for itself in shallow layers of soil and moss. It was more of a suggestion of a walk now, and like us, clung tenaciously to its original purpose in life. What would our guardian angel say about the claims of nature upon us? Her statue, tall and ancient, inhabited the small circled walk, imprisoned in Liriope Muscari and aggressive English ivy, and adorned by tiny stone flowers tucked among her moss covered robes. She was visible from our front porch, but invisible everywhere else, as if she were a secret and holy sentinel sent to guard and bless this place. How long had our human gaze fallen upon that weathered face, worn now by wind and rain and a thousand storms, how many eyes like mine looked at her, and how many more would follow, standing on this porch in the holy stillness of it. I knew one thing, the world was a colder place when I went beyond this land, reached the black ribbon of asphalt leading to town and beyond. But, today, I was ready to venture out. It was time, and she sent me away smiling. I watched her recede, and her goodwill attached itself to me. I felt it all the way to town, and all the way down the long winding country roads through Mississippi until I reached the end of the road where it dissolved into the sea.

Doll Baby and I were taking a trip together, down to the pale sand and blue splendors of the Gulf. She was adorably portable and slept on and off the whole way, finally deciding to be hungry on

Highway 41 at Hattiesburg. We were on our first ever road-trip, a journey of two unequal reasons...to see a friend and selfishly, the Gulf. It had been such a long time. The first sight of it, as we rolled in on Highway 49, took my breath away. What explanation could there be for the power of this place. I was thinking that when I pulled up to the Bay Water in our shiny new car that Whit insisted on buying for me before he went away. Rutledge men were compulsive about cars and trucks, anything with an engine and wheels. The engine was still running when Myra flung herself against the door, opening it before I even had a chance, and I knew right then this trip was the right thing to do. Myra hadn't chosen motherhood, but instead had a serious job in operations that allowed her to have a small apartment on the property back among the pools and cottages and oak trees.

-Come on, she said. Let's get you two situated.

She was married, as I was, to another pilot from our same flight-school class, Phil, but her affections clearly lay right here. I could see that. Two hours later, we were not only situated, but into a second glass of wine, and she had plenty to talk about.

—I don't think it's going to work out with me and Phil. I'm just not cut out to be a military wife. I'm already tired of being lonely, and he'll be gone almost all the time. You know me.

When she used a tone like that, I knew she was being serious. I looked at her sitting there crosslegged, piled up against the sofa cushions with her long dark hair and a face with no emotion.

— What are you going to tell him?

— I'm not going to tell him anything right now, not in a letter. I won't do that, but after he gets back, I'll do it then. I know what he'll say, that we should give it time, that we can work things out. But, I'm not moving into Base Housing on some boring military post and spend my days going to coffees and teas and making any more hats.

The hats…I had almost forgotten about them. We didn't wear hats much in Fontaine, but on an Army post, hats were as vital then as the right amount of starch in fatigues and faultlessly shined boots.

I remembered now. The memory came back to me. Early in our days of flight school, while our husbands were busy mastering level flight and autorotations, Myra and I were mastering the decorum required of officers wives. This included weekly coffee's usually hosted by the Battalion commander's wife and covered protocol for various events. Most of these affairs required a tailored dress, high heels, gloves and a hat. Later on, these rules would become obsolete, but in 1968, they were etched in stone. I had to admit that frankly, I loved the whole thing, the dressing up, the socials, the comfortable predictability of it all. Ask me to host a coffee and I was in heaven. I made petit-fours dripping in pink frosting adorned with green frosting leaves and served coffee from the silver pot I got as a wedding gift. I arranged tall pink gladiolas in my grandmother's cut glass vase. I was completely at home. This was something I understood. So, I was very excited when Major Rawlings wife, Eleanor, announced that for the next month, we would be making hats.

We all arrived at her kitchen table prepared with fabric and scissors and hopeful attitudes. She was extraordinary, a marvelous teacher and a marvelous woman. She rose before dawn, and while her husband went off to fly, she went off to the kitchen to arrange the skillets and bowls we used to shape the silhouettes of our creations. An extra large skillet was perfect for a sun hat. A large mixing bowl was perfect for something a little more Audrey Hepburn.

Eleanor was a practical woman, and reminded us that our husbands military salary would be insufficient for expensive hats. So, in true military, can-do fashion, we chose the obvious solution; we made our own. This wasn't some useless hobby. We made these hats to match our ensembles and planned to wear them to an afternoon tea in the General's Garden. So the hat making began. My hat was navy and white with a puffy top that was a little too severe, and I began to feel deeply insecure when I saw some of the other hats. They were actually quite beautiful, and Eleanor was careful to personally encourage each one of us. She might have struggled a little with mine, but it was a good beginning and the first of many I would make after that. Myra's hat was a vision worthy of Scarlett O'Hara, with a wide linen brim tied with pale pink satin ribbon. She looked beautiful in it, but to her it was just a hat, as uninteresting and unimportant as a jar of peanut butter. To me, the hat suggested something a great deal more. It meant arrival. It meant acceptance in a world where I truly wanted to belong. Maybe some guests at the General's Tea would notice it.

— Who is the attractive lady over there in that striking navy hat? they might say.

— Why, that's Lieutenant Rutledge's wife of course, someone would answer, nodding approval.

I thought about hats and their possible association with Whit's personal advancement. The first beginnings, the whole fantasy made me smile. This was a life I was going to enjoy. Myra... not so much.

Parked on my beach towel in the sun the next day, I continued my exploration of the conflicted characters in my book. The imaginary characters were, in reality, a little too close to Myra and Phil. The distance between them, the coldness, the closed faces that, one day, just didn't feel anything. How did it come to that? Could two people just fall out of love, resent or even begin to hate each other? What if it happened to Whit and me? What if he just announced to me one day that he was unhappy? The unknown was such an unfriendly place, full of dark suspicions that lingered and haunted the minds deep recesses where I was unable to retrieve and examine them in a more benevolent light. I began to dissolve slowly in the soothing warmth, semi-baked in the comforting winds off the Gulf while the sun surrounded me, sinking deep into my bones. I thought my vague, drifting beach thoughts, indistinct questions that never quite succeeded in any quest for answers, as if the sea, that siren of ambiguity, compelled the relinquishment of my demands, submerging reality's hard edges beneath the white froth of each arriving wave.

I peered over the edge of the book at Isabel entertaining herself on the quilt with bright bits of plastic, and it was enough to just be here with her, at peace and not tormented by the ghosts that haunt marriages. But, as I thought about Myra and Phil, I remembered those poor boys who received "Dear John" letters after they had been gone only weeks or months. They lived for mail call and letters from home. Too often, their forever girlfriends were unable to survive even briefly without male companionship, and eventually sat down to write the dreaded letters that all began, "Dear _____, I've met someone else. I'm sorry to break up with you, but it really is for the best ..." or some verbiage like that. Devastation followed and it took weeks or months for young soldiers to get over it. The girl's picture was removed from the door of the soldiers locker, the picture he idolized and looked at every day for encouragement. Her letters, so carefully collected and worn from being read over and over were thrown in the trash. Every reminder would be gone except the memory of her, and that couldn't be so easily disposed of. That was a tough thing to kill, and it lingered for what could seem like an eternity. One of their worst fears was getting a letter like that. I had seen it a few times in other boys Whit knew, that dejected look, the down trodden face of someone who looked like they had lost their best friend. We were always unfailingly kind to those boys, and hoped that eventually life would be kind to them, too.

I gathered up Isabel and wandered back over to the Bay Water, picking my way along the path in the shadows through the oaks, heavy with moss. The cool shade wrapped us like a blanket, and hunger found us in the refrigerator pulling out Isabel's jars of baby food. Later on, Myra took me on a tour, meandering along the office corridors, through the expanse of the lobby and elegant dress shop and ending in the satisfying atmosphere of the restaurant. It was still and quiet. Most of the diners had been lured away now by the blue pools to bask in the sun. We talked about marriage, its ups and downs and wondered what would it be like if we had married someone else. Myra's past contained the usual remnants.

— There was this one boy I knew in college. He was from New Orleans, wore monogrammed shirts and drove one of those vintage station wagons with wood panels on the doors.

They apparently marinated themselves in the many gems of the French Quarter, hung out in the blues clubs and drank Old Fashioned's at Vic's overlooking the river.

— I could have married him, she said. I'm not really sure why I didn't.

Maybe it was that thing women succumb to so often, a man

in uniform. There was Phil, all starched pilot material, dazzling her with his brass, and planting himself firmly in her world until she couldn't exactly think straight. All that was a good while ago though, and I asked Myra what she really wanted now. She sat back in her chair, looked around the elegant atmosphere of the Royal Terrace, its view full of light, the waiters all attention in their crisp white and hesitated. She answered me finally, lightly spreading her hands apart.

— This, this is what I want. I love this world. I love my job and I'm not giving it up.

— What about Phil? Do you love him at all? Does he love you?

— I don't know for sure. I think we liked the romance of it, the feeling that in the whole wide world, it was just us, and we were the only ones who really understood each other. We held hands over dinner and talked about having a cabin in the Smokies with a view of the valley when the leaves turn all gold and red. His sister says I'm the sister she always wanted.

— So, what happened?

— One day, sometime during flight school, it just seemed like he became a whole different person. I woke up one morning and felt like I didn't know him at all.

We both sat back and slipped into just being girls talking like we used to and thought about old times; who we were then and who we are now, and we ate our Bay Water Sandwiches with their perfect sauce. The waiters hovered inconspicuously around us, fulfilling our every expectation, apparently impervious to the continuous misfortunes of women. They refilled our iced tea, plied us with dessert and we talked some more. Or, I let her talk some more. That's what friends do when a life hangs in the balance.

The next morning we all got up a little slow, mostly because we could and it felt good. Myra had plans to entertain Isabel while I went off on my own.

—Go on, get out of here. God knows you need some time by yourself. Motherhood has made you real uptight, she said with a laugh.

So, I drove away alone for the first time in a long time, into a clear morning framed by white sand and skies of bluest blue. Time blurred when driving the coast. Reality became smaller and smaller, withdrawing until the shining waves of the Gulf became all there was on this earth. I made my way through the slow miles of this watery otherworld all the way to The Pass and turned around there, past the neat rows of white sail boats asleep in the harbor rocking in gentle unison on almost imperceptible waves. I headed back to the east on the grey ribbon of road, the artery edged in blue and white that became a kind of destiny of its own; easy to follow, easy to feel. It led on through Long Beach toward Gulfport, the rising silhouettes of the Port and the Yacht Club just visible now against the long slate blue horizon. I thought then about stopping for lunch, so I turned into the long drive that lead to the water, parked and walked into the vintage gray building facing the sea.

It was exactly as I remembered, rustic and nautical, gray with bravery and decorum, and the faces of small, freckled children over at the side window asked the barman for lemonade. I sat alone at one of the small tables out on the porch with a view of the Gulf and ate a hamburger, my favorite thing here. Every bite was a taste of heaven. Feeling a little reckless, I threw caution to the winds and even ordered champagne from the bar. It was crisp and cold and made me smile, wondering what the good people in Fontaine would say if they could see me now, drinking in public in the middle of the day. The sensation was deliciously rebellious, and I drank it slowly, savoring it, trying to make the moment last. Drawn, like always, to the predestined waves arriving now, connected to other worlds by an unbroken sea, I was saved again, sitting on this porch by the waters of the Gulf, its flat smooth islands of advancing beach now laid bare by the tide low and receding, breaking far out against the permanent edges of the sky. The waves I remembered from past days, my other life here, were an occupying presence, as I was myself on the white sand of this place that claimed me. The soft crashing sound floated invisible in the breeze, always with a kindness to it, an ease soft and warm that melted like liquid moonlight against ink blue when night came. A hundred transcendent moments like this drifted effortlessly on currents that did their invisible work, as they had for years and lifetimes. Every breath changed me until there was no place except this place, and I was safe in its arms. There was unspeakable comfort in thinking, "here I did this and this," walked the same steps, the same beach, the same ground. And out beyond the ribbon of sand, light in broken shards reflected on the long edges of the sea, tranquil beacons of the waves rising as the waters made their slow return again, and there was reassurance in the constancy of it.

That was when I saw them. They came into my view from just down the beach, two figures walking the slow unhurried walk of people happy with the feel of bare feet on warm sand. Their faces were indistinct, too far away to really see, but the wind swept through her long dark hair, and she reached up to brush back the loose strands from her face. Her companion was tall and young and strong and moved with the casualness of someone who was completely at ease here. They drifted, hesitantly at times, both looking out at the sky, she leaning against him lightly, the way people do who are comfortable with each other and there is nothing left to say or prove. They looked quite young, maybe nineteen or twenty. Something in the way they stood there, the way they moved toward each other, then apart, made me think this no careless romantic stroll, no casual walk on the beach in the warmth of approaching noon when the cool of morning has already slipped away. No, it was not that. It looked like good-bye, and I could feel small hints of regret settling in and mingling with the winds off the Gulf. I observed them together as one does passers-by at a sidewalk cafe, watching people, how they talk, how they move, how they dress and wondering what their lives are like. These were clearly not children, but there was an innocence about them that made me think their childhood was not so long ago. The cares of the world did not cling to them now and it surely would later. Today it was only the two of them on this beach as if nothing and no one else existed at all. They drifted finally away from me, their slow aimless steps taking them farther down the beach toward Biloxi, and I wondered, was he a Biloxi boy and was she a Gulfport girl? Were they two star-crossed lovers unable to overcome the opposition of parents and families who moved in directions that were poles apart?

My fingers felt cold now, chilled by the pale champagne cool against the edges of the glass, and I set it down on the table to look at the soothing bubbles rising up in long narrow streams. For this one small moment my life was inordinately simple, just the Gulf and me and tiny trails of tinted, predictable bubbles confined to a transparent cylinder, all gilt framed by natant blue. If only I hadn't seen them, I thought. If only they hadn't walked down that beach at that moment, then I wouldn't have remembered. Part of me wanted to remember the past, when that slight figure walking along the white beach was me. I was that girl standing there looking out at those gossamer waves just like the girl with the long dark hair and he was there beside me reaching out for my hand in that casual way we thought would last forever. Myra had her boy from college, and someone lingered in my past, too. He was twenty-four and working on his Masters. We were summer lifeguards together, happy and golden brown in the way that people are who have been around a pool everyday in full summer sun. Hayes was from a ranching family and his aspirations lay firmly with his predecessors on the ranges of Wyoming, the storied west of cowboys and exhilarating freedom splashed wide against mountain grandeur and luminous valleys drenched in the green and gold of spring.

 I pushed back my chair from the table and turned slightly where I could better see the Gulf. The other guests were gone now, back to their jobs and lives and thoughts of supper and PTA and ball games. I didn't mind that I was here alone now. I settled back, asked for some coffee and looked out at the Gulf, my favorite thing. If only one or two things had been different, I wouldn't be sitting here right now numbed by the soothing waves and the pleasing effects of champagne. No, I wouldn't be here. I would be wearing boots and jeans, tending horses and busy planning for the next rodeo, breathing crisp mountain air, occupied by stock and hay prices and wondering just how bad the next winter might be. I sat here in the safe haven of the Yacht Club, looking out into infinity with my hands around my warm cup of coffee and tried to imagine it, a picture of life with my cowboy framed against the "purple mountain's majesty" famously written about in 1893. One afternoon's walk on a beach, one simple decision, and everything about my life would have been different.

I wanted to come out to Wyoming with him right then that summer to see it, his rugged kingdom of staggering elevations and cows and horses grazing the grass filled range before the early snows came. But, Hayes said that spring would be better, that I would love watching the earth come alive. That was our moment, his and mine. I would have come home engaged. But instead, we went off in different directions to different schools and the end came more suddenly than I could have imagined. I met Whit and everything changed. Hayes's grandfather died suddenly and he went home to the sympathetic warmth of friends and neighbors, one of whom was a fair haired girl whose qualities he failed to appreciate in the eighth grade. She had, I think, become a Rodeo Queen. We both found ourselves living now in an unforeseen future that was so different from the one we imagined that summer.

 I finally got up and walked out of the safe shadows of the Yacht Club toward the parking lot, out of the comfortable past, leaving parts of myself in this liquid sanctuary as I always did, fragments of my life scattered like bread crumbs on warm sand. My fat, brown pelican friends were not here to say hello or good-bye. I remembered them clustered on the empty posts of every vacant pier later in the year, roosting then everywhere and skimming in tight bombardier formations along the water like feathered members of an Ornithological Convention. I missed seeing their fluffy brown silhouettes, and my familiar memories of them came back with me all the way to north Mississippi. I drove east in the afternoon warmth along the beach road to the Bay Water, back to real life, back to Isabel and Myra. She had Doll Baby down for a nap and was almost asleep on the sofa herself. She said she didn't realize how much fun babies were and they were both entirely worn out. It was good to see her really smile. Isabel had worked her little magic. Later on, we decided to do dinner and a movie, so I left Doll Baby with a high school baby sitter employed for the specific purpose of catering to the needs of hotel guests. She promised me Isabel was in experienced hands, at least as experienced as a sixteen year old can be. She had been babysitting her younger brothers since she was thirteen, so I was staring at three years of feeding and diapering and baby bouncing. She seemed capable and came with excellent references. I thought a tiny second about calling her English teacher to inquire about her study skills and whether she could string two sentences together. I was inclined to judge people by their ability to conjugate verbs and spell basic words like "conjugate." Finally, Myra and I slipped away to dinner and a movie while Isabel was distracted by her pop-up clown box. It played "Pop Goes the Weasel," over and over and over. She loved that.

    I couldn't remember the last time I was out in the evening as a single person. It felt strange and good all at the same time, a little like being a college girl again. Myra turned out onto the beach road in her little convertible and we headed for The Wharf, a rustic and rambling domain perched on stilts overlooking the water. It was where the locals ate, not like the tourist places further down in Biloxi that catered to rowdy singles looking for action. It was known locally for fresh seafood right off of the boat and famous for its Mystery Pie, a divine concoction whose recipe was a closely held secret. Dinner began with a massive tray of oysters on the half shell buried in ice, and then we were up to our elbows in crab and fried shrimp, all the offerings of the Gulf in their perfection. We ate while the sun sank further and further down into the Gulf, talked nonsense about the current, really short skirt length, smokey eye shadow, the new bellbottoms and watched the boats out in the channel. Then we settled on going over to Lettie Mae's for drinks and to the Late Show in Gulfport to see a newish movie appropriately titled, "How to Save a Marriage and Ruin Your Life." It was a bubbly, romantic romp perfect for young women like us who craved double-buttered popcorn, the movie theater kind that we were always trying to duplicate at home. The pretty picture of hopelessly attractive men and flawlessly beautiful women unencumbered by anything more than love and lust filled the screen with lavish images designed to capture our attention, and at this moment it served as a kind anesthetic, not unlike like dime bags of marijuana or mind numbing amounts of alcohol or recklessly shopping or driving at ridiculous speeds or binge-watching television. It was an escape, a diversion, anything to ease the pain of loneliness and separation even for a little while. It reminded me of a quote I read somewhere, "The pursuit of an antidote for despair can lead down many roads, some more attractive than others."

We mingled with the audience filtering slowly up the aisles, left the theater that night and went home, but Hollywood definitely did not go home with us. The audience was mainly women, many from Keesler Air Force Base in Biloxi and some from the Navy and Coast Guard stations nearby. For us, the waiting young military wives, home was as different as it could be from the frothy on-screen illusion. Ours was a grayed reality of aggregate edges where neither love nor lust nor men existed at all, or maybe would ever exist again. We lived in a narrowing demilitarized zone, imprisoned by the hard borders of hope and reality, an in-between place of obscured identities and undefined forgetfulness. Moving in it everyday seemed more like sleep walking, a dreamlike state where nothing was too real. It was important to keep that feeling at bay, that feeling of realness. There was too much visceral pain in it, too much to bear. But, sometimes it crept in against our wills and there it was to deal with. Despair was such an ugly thing. There was no pity in it, and it only ended in tears that fell hot and salty, ran down our cheeks and ruined our mascara. That face in the mirror wet with the long liquid black streaks was something to be avoided if at all possible. Getting over it was way too hard. Grief, that relentless companion of despair and insidious thief of joy, had a tenacity that surprised me. It equaled the unequivocal assault of combat, a war waged in my mind, in all our minds, and from the very beginning, dogged, continuous resistance was our only weapon against it.

We drove back to the resort, cruising with the top down, open to the Gulf air of a dark night luminous with stars, and for just a minute Myra and I were girls again, young and carefree, the warm salt wind blowing our hair. We might have been college coeds in the casual breeze of a Saturday night with all the other cars full of young faces, laughing about boyfriends, dates and getting back to the dorm late after some party. The headline in the Biloxi paper that day read, "Students Arrested in Violent March," but apparently none of those students were down here. They were in Boston or Ann Arbor or some other hotbed of protest, and we were safe in the blessed arms of a congenial South where we settled our differences in other ways. At least we weren't surrounded by unsympathetic people. There was comfort of a sort here among our own, a palpable feeling of good will that permeated the air we breathed. It had a kind of salvation in it, maybe left over from some ancient brush arbor revivals that elicited the highest order of sanctity, the kind that spread out like warm butter over souls and everyone was better for it. I remembered hearing about those from older relatives. Country people came from miles away to camp out for days to hear some traveling preacher. How much we took for granted now. How much good will was sown in those hard days that fell to earth and took root for such times as these. There really was no name for what that was, but we all knew it, recognized it, and I never felt it anywhere else.

Isabel was a sleeping angel when we got back to Myra's apartment hibernating in her port-a-crib, a collapsible bed ingeniously designed for traveling with babies. She had that great gift of all infants, an unawareness of struggle, of loneliness, of discord of any kind. She slept through it all and woke each morning a cheerful and effervescent cherub ready to spread her rosy joy all over everybody. I lay there for a long time on Myra's sofa bed before I drifted off, my eyes wide open in the darkness, listening to Isabel's soft breaths, shifting among innocent memories of luminous days and warm sand, still seeing Whit's faded image, half smiling, framed there against a blue Gulf. Morning finally came for us all, its perfect golden haze full of promise. I gathered up Isabel, and we left Myra, the Bay Water and the soft white beach early, driven north into the tall pines by salty winds off the Gulf and made our pilgrimage to the other place that anchored us. Later, threading through the forests and farms of names like Mount Olive and Winona and Grenada, in the faded, shining hours beyond the waves and the light and the warm sand against my skin, all the way across the changing landscape, I remained comfortably absorbed in that luminous world, disarming and permanent. It was there all the way north to Fontaine. The Gulf had come home with us…or maybe we had come home with it. I ate our last buttered biscuit in Yalobusha County under a frosted canopy of cottony clouds and green pines framed like a portrait against a stark blue Mississippi sky. We were missed at the farm, even though we hadn't even left Mississippi. When we drove in, Peach saw us coming from the porch and couldn't get Doll Baby into her waiting arms fast enough. And, as I stepped out onto Whit's ground, I saw our angel emerging like an amiable concierge among the bursting blooms of wild violets scattered at her feet in wide serpentine clusters that had come to greet us, to welcome us home.

CHAPTER SIX

"OUR TOWN"

—∞—

In many ways, the story, *Our Town* laid the foundation for stories about small towns, and Fontaine had all the elements to belong in that class. It practically begged to be immortalized in prose. Even I could see that from the first time I laid eyes on it. I saw it first from the east looking toward the river, the sun behind us casting morning light on the church spires and tall victorian houses dripping in gingerbread. Whit brought me home to this place, newly married, and hoped I would love it. I did. Our town sat on raised sandstone bluffs hugging the Nunnehi River, Cherokee for "The Immortals," named by the small band of Cherokee that camped here long ago before drifting on to the north east near Tunica. Once riverboats brought people and provisions to this place until time and catastrophe and the calculations of the universe changed everything, leaving the remains of some extravagant dreams and the foundation of our town, newly minted civilization, in its place. That it existed at all was a triumph. An explorer and trapper, Gaubert August de la Fontaine fought his way through the wilderness of canebrakes and marshes stretching east from the Mississippi River into the unspoiled vastness that became Fontaine County. The emerging community survived in spite of floods, war, Reconstruction, the great cholera epidemic of 1854 and the devastation of cotton by the boll weevil in 1900. The town was a testament to survivors and to the human spirit bent on sustaining a new life clinging tenaciously to fertile ground beyond the bluffs. Its population now hovered at 29,000 souls, most of whom had been here for generations and whose predecessors now lay at eternal repose in Fernwood, guarded by sweeping branches and wrought iron and spirits of the Immortals lent to us by those who once occupied this ground.

Perfectly square, Fontaine sat in long blocks around its main thoroughfare, Washington Street, in honor of our first president. An alarming number of churches anchored almost every corner, built as if an insufficient number of altars might fail to accomplish the spiritual atonement of the residents who were even now precariously clinging to the invisible boundaries of eternity. "Knocking on the doors of Heaven," was the phrase used most often to describe the aged, or sometimes the wayward person whose church attendance, or lack of it, was evidence of an unrepentant heart and an indication of lax attention to the spiritual realms. Surrounding these citadels of divinity, stately homes on long leafy streets announced their authority to everyone. Equal stars in this universe of southern architecture, their rising facades, front porches dripping hospitality, encrusted columns and ornamented dormers on Beauregard Avenue made Fontaine equal almost to Natchez. People here were proud of that, and especially proud of the grand street of larger homes styled after Stanton Hall, Windsor or Choctaw Hall with their wide lawns rimmed by azaleas cascading in pink and white over omniscient, Virgilian boundaries of scrolled iron suggesting that they pre-dated God.

Whit dropped me into this world in the casual way that boys and men often do, hopeful that assimilation will occur, relationships will be established and a life can be built together.

The reality is a little more complicated. At our first social event at the country club, I was essentially the reluctant star of a one act play where the heroine, me, was performing for the first time to a sold-out but somewhat dubious audience. Questions were asked. Eyebrows were raised.

— Where did he find her? Who are her people? You know he could have married one of our local girls.

People would wonder about that for a long time. If you weren't from here, belonging was something that took time, maybe a long time. But the real truth was that most of these folks made their first baby steps right here in the venerable vastness of this clubby room, and their great grand-daddy was a founding member who laid out the fairways and greens of the lush landscape viewed from the cooling verandas with their wide black and white striped awnings. My white high heels stood on consecrated ground and there was no mistaking the power circulating in the room between all the people who authentically belonged here. Thankfully, I wore pale pink nail polish and an impeccably fitted white sheathe dress, just enough to make a statement, tasteful and almost impossible to criticize. We arrived with his parents who were like God's gifts to me. All smiling and animated, they introduced me around, and I got the feeling that people thought if I was okay with Whitney and Cynthia, then I was okay with them. This was my first introduction to living in herds. You move when the flock moves. You sense danger and hesitate when it hesitates, like an orchestrated dance rhythmically moving in sedate circles to silent music unheard outside of these hallowed walls. I saw these same people again and again in our town. Greetings became more familiar, more cordial, and I was introduced now as Cynthia's daughter-in-law, a sort of title that conferred acceptance, and everything in me wanted to live and move in this perfect picture of pleasantness.

So, that was how I came here for the first time, and now that I had returned, living at the farm with Isabel, these were still my people. Whit was one of their own, and I had mostly been forgiven for stealing away "one of our boys" from some local girl whose momma had her eye on Whit since kindergarten as a future son-in law. Some things died hard, or not at all, and every now and then that issue was raised at some party or tea or chance meeting in the department store. An otherwise sweet matron would see me, pause and make a slow turn, fixing her steely eye on me as if I had stolen her membership to the Daughters of the Old South. Then she brought up the circumstance that she still found so irritating.

— You know Martha Ann and Whit were always sweet on each other ever since their sixth grade class picnic. However did you manage to steal him away from our girls?

Well, I always just smiled back and said I didn't know how in the world that happened and I hoped Martha Ann would find someone real soon who appreciated a pretty girl like her. That helped some, but these matrons could be forgetful or maybe just a teeny bit vengeful, like I needed to be reminded of my transgression. I would like to have said something that irritated her right back.

— You know, Mrs. Dalton, the truth is Whit and I spent a considerable amount of time in the back seat of his car, and after that he started to find Martha Ann boring. I knew that was a bad thing to say or even think, and it certainly wasn't true, but I thought it might have sounded good.

Some days I took Isabel to the stores downtown on Washington Street that supplied all the needs and most of the wants for just about everyone, or we went right out on the edge of town to the Rebel Dip where they served the best Chicken in a Basket in the county and soft serve ice cream. Isabel loved it. I spoon fed it to her but it still got all over her nice, clean, floral print baby dresses somehow. Darlene pretty much always got our food for us. She was another native, a through and through descendant of these parts, dressed in the identifying holy gray of the Confederacy. The giant rectangular sign on top of the Rebel Dip had a picture of a Kentucky Colonel in his wide hat waving a Confederate flag, and both waitresses wore gray uniforms with little bitty, pin-on Confederate flags. The Rebel Dip was a local institution. Everybody came here, and on Sundays they had to put on three waitresses to handle all the church people who came to eat their fried Chicken in a Basket. It came always hot right out of the grease with a small pot of honey on the side to dip every tasty morsel in. It was heaven, and they had bottomless blueberry pie, made by Mr. Wade himself, who had been baking pies with his momma since he could hold a rolling pin. Sometimes, he came out of the kitchen to visit with "the customers." His own son, Lyle, was in Viet Nam near Pleiku, so we always talked about what we had heard last. Lyle was in the Army, patrolling the formidable and contested grounds deep in the jungles and subject to some of the worst fighting. Mr. Wade's story was always worse than mine, so I tried to make mine seem bad too, so he wouldn't feel like Lyle was suffering and other boys weren't.

He and Darlene were a good fit. She worked for him for thirteen years right out of high school, and her brother Ray Don was just back from Viet Nam with his own problems and needed a job and a shoulder to cry on. Like many, so many of our boys, he was just so young and away from home for the first time. He'd never even been out of the county, never been anywhere, not even to Memphis. His brother bragged, and was still bragging, that he had been all the way to the lobby of the Peach Tree. I think that was the extent of his travels, eclipsing everyone else in his family except his parents who, one October, in a rare moment of extreme enthusiasm, drove all the way to the Mississippi State Fair in Jackson. Ray Don had shrapnel wounds from a grenade and saw his best friend blown into bits beside him, and he was shaken clear through. Everyone could see it. Something never quite settled within him, and folks here who had no reference at all to the actualities of the war wondered what was, "wrong with Ray Don." They expected, I thought, for the boys who came home from Viet Nam to behave like the soldiers returning from World War II, who eased back into family life and seemed unscathed by it all. My own father and uncles who fought, never mentioned it, never talked about it at all, and I was too young to even guess why.

Ray Don limped around on his bad leg, with pain that never seemed to completely go away, and languished over his lost girlfriend who didn't want to marry "a cripple." He tried to get a job down at the gas station but Mr. Dean the owner, said he didn't think Ray Don could move fast enough to gas up a car and clean the windshield and check under the hood. People didn't like to be kept waiting. So, Mr. Wade gave him odd jobs out at the Rebel Dip. That was the thing about Mr. Wade I liked. He was what some people referred to as the salt of the earth. He bounced Doll Baby on his lap and worried over Lyle and consoled Darlene and baked pies all at the same time. He hadn't been to church in over twenty years because all those church people expected to be fed on Sunday, and he could almost make a whole week's worth of income just on that one day. When he did "practice his faith," it was usually praying for Lyle or Ray Don, and his sanctuary wasn't the hushed house of God on one of the many holy corners in town. It was back in the kitchen over hot grease frying up chicken. Maybe God heard those prayers more, the ones born of desperation. I hoped He heard mine.

We were assaulted often here in our little womb of consolation, too often, by jarring scenes from far off places like New York where in March, throngs of hippies took over Grand Central Station in what was originally something called a "be-in" that turned quickly into a raw anti-war protest. Dressed in hippie bell bottoms, tie-dye, fringe and headbands, the youthful protesters swayed back and forth, arm in arm, chanting the revolutionary songs of El Commandante right there in black and white on the nightly news. I could almost hear Whitney and R. J. muttering for the hundredth time, "Who the hell are these people?" There were now, in descending order, categories of individuals previously unknown to us; Hippies and Yippies sandwiched between the feminists and revolutionaries, all gripped in the unstoppable momentum of a sweeping movement celebrating free love and acid rock. It was a lot to digest. The press became the PR department for a "new generation" with a new morality. The "Peace-swarm" of 1968 confidently announced a sexual revolution that would redefine American culture, obliterating families as expressions of oppression and encouraging young people to free themselves from these inconvenient moral shackles by turning on and tuning out. Here in Fontaine, we found this troubling to say the least. If they could successfully occupy Grand Central Station on national TV, what other American bastions would be the next to fall. Who were these people, these hippies, anyway? Was wearing flowers in their hair and sleeping with anyone and everyone under the forgiving stars of California something that demanded imitation? Apparently so, because every newscast brought it a little closer to us. It was as if America's young people had lost their collective minds and revolution was the only thing they talked about or cared about. Except here in the South. We rarely saw it here. The bonds of family were too strong, and though there might have been a few among us that hungered for revolution, sleeping in the streets of Haight-Ashbury or meditating in an ashram at the feet of some illuminated Yogi, we mostly looked at the confusing onslaught with suspicion, as we would a misplaced and unfamiliar stranger.

Fontaine fell among the ascending towns along the river, the region attracting commerce, and hopefully, more of it. It was essentially run by four or five ruling families who owned banks and businesses, sat on the city council, ran for mayor and managed the upward direction of our emerging metropolis. They all lived on the hallowed ground of Beauregard Avenue and we all understood the hierarchy inherent in this arrangement. When encountered, they were accorded the reverential attentiveness required by their position. No one questioned this, or objected to it, not for a hundred years. I managed to meet one day, and become friends with two venerable residents of Beauregard Avenue, Miss Agatha and Miss Fannie, ancient sisters who might have been actual saints. They were petite and nearly identical, with small gold spectacles and dainty embroidered handkerchiefs smelling faintly of orris-root.

A large canon from the War of Northern Aggression decorated their impeccable front lawn encircled by a bed of lavender petunia's. It was retrieved by some now deceased relative, they said, near Brice's Crossroads, from ground made famous by the Battle of Guntown. Confederate troops, gallantly fighting on ground wet after days of rain, routed the invading northern forces who fled in wild retreat over six counties retiring at last in Memphis. North Mississippi saw its share of blood and battles and rationing, and posted the lists of the newly dead on the gray facades of courthouses where everyone gathered in the hushed anticipation of grief.

Over the years, at the rear of the sprawling house, the sisters and their aged gardener planted roses and boxwoods in severe rectangles around the aging statue of an eponymous angel, wings and hands in repose as if lost in prayer, prayers joined by Miss Agatha and Miss Fannie each morning as they took tea on the veranda. They prayed for each other and for the souls of the lost, and even for the souls of the dead, rocking gentle and determined in the bottle green wicker chairs of their youth. Their beloved brother Asa was sadly departed, resting now in the leafy arms of Fernwood, leaving them, two spinsters, alone in their massive house with only a cook, a maid and a gardener who also drove them about in a silver, vintage 1942 touring car. They would undoubtedly join him soon, all resting together, at peace in the family plot on the edges of eternity.

How they carried on, given their sheltered background, was a mystery to me, but they managed to be bright and shining stars in a dark universe, full of Christian benevolence and lavish warmth that rivaled any that I had ever known. They were serious and devout Bible people, children of missionary parents in the dark recesses of China in the days where survival there was possible, and that history marked them forever. To enter their home was a transforming experience, and they were among the figures that stood out in the small universe of Fontaine for me, and I'm sure, for others. They were members of a staid, main-line church, the old kind of Christians with fortitude that matched their convictions, and Sunday after Sunday they occupied their family pew at First Church down on the corner of Washington, possibly one of the holier locations among a litany of others. They quietly did their good deeds, advocating modesty and perseverance, qualities at odds with the onslaught of decadence daily descending upon us, and thus made their mark upon the world, a world I felt was just a tad unworthy of them. Holiness, that word so bandied about, what did it look like really? Were we actually capable of it, or was the Bible just a book full of pious talk that made everyone feel pleasantly holy without actually having to do anything? If holiness was possible, the ancient sisters certainly had it.

They were ports in a storm, Miss Agatha and Miss Fannie. Surely they had been girls once, wanted suitors and flower bouquets and homes and children with ribbons in their hair and a thousand dreams recognized in the warm arms of an adoring lover. Had they ever been kissed? Did they know the loss when a suitor slipped away out of reach forever, watching him walk away into a future without her in it, or receive the letter, the one all women dread, that he was gone, swallowed up by death and nothing could bring him back? How much grief had they known between the two of them? I suspected, a lot. But, they had born it well and lived now with carefully managed memories. Somehow, they had done it. The latest war in jungles far away brought us together, the sisters and me, the inescapable scepter of death always close around us, and we watched daily for The List as women from all wars have done.

Death visited Joseph P. Hall's family in Texas and Rudy Johnson's mother in Nebraska. Young men from Georgia and Montana died together, their names added to the expanding inventory of the fallen. We all felt it, the same sorrow that arrived in every state and city and village with every war, the carnage sent to try us all, to see what we were made of. Every obituary, every reminder of loss stirred deep grief, another tragedy to face that lived in the printed news pages and merely recorded facts, revealing nothing of the torn emotional fragments left behind. American women were not strangers to adversity. From our earliest days, we built and baked and plowed the fields, and moved on to clear and plant and raise children in some new wilderness, often dying along the way, buried in obscurity on an unmarked trail under Mississippi live oaks or Texas cottonwoods or Kentucky hickory. Out here, commiseration was a commodity originally dispensed long ago, throughout the length and breadth of this land with compassionate and gently gloved hands. Now, centuries later, we were all still doing it.

CHAPTER SEVEN

THE EMPIRE OF THE LIVING

Bourbon, that elixir of the gods and panacea of good will, elicits from observers both praise and condemnation, depending almost entirely on a point of view perhaps established in childhood or etched in stone from the earliest days of Sunday School. Its reputation for being hard liquor lumped it unfortunately all together with the other alcoholic beverages demonized long before the days of prohibition by ardent women of the temperance movement. But, among its admirers, no conversation adequately proceeded without congenial references to the provenance of the sacred mash bill, proofs and barrels. This cornucopia of knowledge was usually acquired through drinking copious amounts that lead through an alcohol nuanced maze to a lifetime of acquired expertise. I discovered all of this by simply sitting under Ilene's oak trees or on her expansive screened-in front porch. She preferred a deeply American spirit with a wheated history first offered back in 1870 by its imaginative and forward thinking creator. Perhaps my tastes, undeveloped and unsophisticated, simply lead me down a likely path, the one less traveled that, "diverged in the yellow wood." I merely sipped, occasionally and briefly, having yet to acquire the skill and appreciation for the subtle nuances demanded by an authentic and ardent connoisseur

Ilene's friends were rather like a brotherhood of educated bandits, and they were quietly unapologetic about their preferences for just about everything. Discussions among them might cover any subject under the sun, but the favorite and dearest to their heart was literature. Throw out luminaries from the Renaissance or anyone French and they were in literary Heaven, already on holy ground speaking the language of angels. Mention *De l'Esprit des lois (The Spirit of Law)* or *Candide* and prepare to sit quietly listening for at least an hour. These monuments to persuasion fortified their essential bent toward freedom of thought, a position not to be taken lightly. That I was invited down occasionally to a discussion sérieuse was due to Ilene's generosity and largess. She felt strongly that I needed to get out of the house more and was always looking for ways to both advance my intellectual development and bathe me in the warm comforts of genteel companionship.

— Here, have some more paté, she would say, and some more crisps. I made these just this morning. You are entirely too thin.

Her bread crisps were crunchy and delicious New Orleans French bread sliced wafer thin and dipped in butter and garlic. They then spent lonely hours in a slow oven before being rescued at the perfect stage of crispness and served warm, the hint of garlic aroma guaranteed to bring us all practically to our knees.

Perhaps it was the primitive influence of the vestigial oaks and antique wicker on Southern soil that fed the group encounters, that and the Bourbon, but there was a palpable connection between cut glass Bourbon glasses, their contents and the level of verbiage on the table. Ilene had the excellent foresight to plan these soiree's around small plates of sustenance that had the mollifying effects of both absorbing the libations and also soothing the tastes and meeting the deepest culinary needs of her guests. Who could resist her Duck Foie Gras among the ancestral oak groves, a pâté eliciting a genteel sort of refinement that soothed the soul and, for a few brief, happy hours, made the world into a much more desirable place. Elevating was how I described it, and it augmented an advanced course in Literature accompanied by the other gastronomical benefits of Bourbon and decadent Escargots à la Bourguignonne. Best of all, I was spared the communal prison of a drab and uninspiring classroom possibly overlooking the horrid flat roof of some adjacent building littered with the skeletons of dead and dying ventilation systems. It was a very different and pleasant form of education. One afternoon was devoted entirely to the emergence of *Cat on a Hot Tin Roof* and *Heart of Darkness*. It was an object lesson in the hollowness of human nature, as were their discussions of other formidable works like *Light in August* and *Absalom, Absalom!* Where else in the world would I hear such things. The guests treated me with the lightness suitable for a young person, acknowledgment but not esteem, not yet. You had to earn that. As for the War, they had a less than favorable impression of it, and the discussions about the folly of young soldiers led to understanding nods about the erstwhile protesters in Berkley and New York. The eloquent exploration of sacrifice and humanity in *For Whom the Bell Tolls* was proof enough of the grim tragedies of foreign wars. If they had all been younger by a few years, I was relatively sure they would be out there right now marching in beards, beads and wearing viva revolución T-shirts themselves.

The least vocal of the group, by miles, was the parish rector, the local ecclesiastical authority and friend to his congregation, Father Ed. Well educated at Sewanee and Edinburgh, he had all the qualities necessary to survive and thrive in the American spiritual wilderness and guide the flock more perfectly in the way. He had a light touch, more so than some of the other local preachers who were not quite as elastic in their points of view. I talked to R. J. a few times about this, and having been formed in the classic evangelical mold, he embraced the unquestioning faith of his fathers. Faith and more of it, led a person deeper in the ways of the Lord. I did quietly wonder if this truly was all there was, and if there was more, where would one go to find it. These were only a few of the questions I had. I did learn that certain churches were dispensationalists, and they believed the age of miracles had passed. Well, I discovered later that other folks disagreed with that. There were churches right down the street who were "laying on hands," and apparently experiencing miracles every night and twice on Sunday. Who knew the expanses of Christendom spread so wide and the fault lines went so deep. My spiritual discontent drew me to Father Ed who was approachable and steady, with singular gray eyes that seemed understanding and wise and capable of humor. He knew his stuff, but apparently his education hadn't rendered him an artificial ecclesiastic trying only to survive the minefields of church politics until a happy retirement near a trout stream in the Appalachians. He radiated an inner warmth without even trying and brought solace to everyone without seeming to exert any effort, and I liked him very much.

Sometimes, after her gathering, Ilene insisted we go downtown to Wells Department store and look at whatever new things had come in that week. Mr. Johnny Wells owned that store, as his father had before him, and he was usually stationed right at the front in the Men's department ready to greet each customer who walked through the door. He knew every person in town by name, their spouse's names, their children's names, their ages, what sports they played and usually who their English teachers were. His greetings were always the jovial, pat-on-the-back type that compelled standing around to talk. Long conversations were wisely encouraged and inevitably resulted in shopping in one or all of the departments on both floors. Always impeccably dressed in the latest suit, coordinated shirt and tie, he presided over his little domaine with the same attentive, solicitous care of an undertaker, looking at the victim/customer with a thoroughly appraising eye and then, at the proper moment, offering thoughtful comments and suggestions.

— Ilene, this new green dress with the full skirt is perfect for you. Try on a size eight, and we just got in the matching shoes and handbag. Margaret, come and help Ilene with those.

Margaret was one of a dozen employees who like several others, had been with him for more than thirty years. They were essentially all family. Some of their predecessors had even worked for Mr. Johnnie's father who was just as capable and just as liked by everyone. The best dressed people in town shopped here, and if they weren't perfectly turned out it reflected poorly on him. He took this very seriously, as if the entire social structure of Fontaine laid heavily on his perfectly attired shoulders. His real specialty was Men's Wear, and I myself heard him, multiple times, correct some local gentleman, suggesting in the most casual way possible that he reconsider those brown shoes, or change the sleeve length on that sport coat. He was really good at what he did, and when he wasn't at the store, he was teaching Sunday School, attending some club meeting or coaching boys baseball.

In some ways, Mr. Johnnie's department store was like a smooth running military headquarters, firmly directing the flow of stabilizing currents running steadily and predictably through the fabric of our small universe. It was part of his job, a sacred duty to outfit his fellows well. An armed outpost of conservatism, armed at least, with suits and ties and dresses and handbags, the store was a haven of respectability with standards understood by everyone. Clothes, appropriate ones, were reflections of ones values, and in Fontaine, values were everything. Other clothes, styles with dubious beginnings had begun arriving on the national scene in 1968, the specious garments of the hippie counterculture and beatnik philosophy. Bell bottoms and fringed vests rode in on a high tide of the new morality, and with it began the era of tie-dye and peace signs, bare midriffs and long hair. This was the new uniform of the age, worn daily by young people in other places, savagely laying waste to the standards of a generation and taking the country by storm. Such styles would not be seen here in Fontaine in any store, nor worn by any respectable person, unless they drifted in clinging to the frame of a visitor from the outside eager to advertise their new found self expression. We saw them from time to time, on some family guest briefly in town and obviously devoted to the cultural war on anything conventional. Although these visitors were not all cut from the same mold, they generally were anti-war, an attitude reflected usually in their long necklaces heavy with beads and peace signs. They seemed to have been more or less swallowed whole by the era, in an unstoppable movement characterized by pot, free love, drug fueled music and movies like *The Graduate* or *I Love You, Alice B. Toklas*.

Here in Fontaine, bell bottoms, that defining accessory of the dissident generation, were never sold in Mr. Johnnie's store, not in 1968. The shaggy, newly minted devotees of Vishnu, chanting to preserve the planet, never darkened the door of this place. And Women's Lib, that hotbed of contention, never found a foothold here in the dress department or any other department, under any circumstances. Protesting the war here seemed un-American, and the New York hippie ways of East Village failed to migrate into the fertile fields and pines of our world in north Mississippi. Maybe we were all just too busy weeding gardens, gathering in summer produce, feeding cows and plowing fields to find discontent under every rock. Or, maybe the elite students displayed nightly on the news, flush with gifts of leisure and education simply found this moment's compelling idealism too alluring to ignore. Whatever the case, we were all stuck with it, and I personally felt a yawning gap so wide between their sensibilities and my own, that it became a bridge too far, uncrossable and foreign. Loyalties became tangible things now, not unlike that of the brave soul courageous enough to whistle bars of La Marseillaise on the German occupied streets of Belgium in 1910. The punishment was death, but loyalty to ones countrymen was a thing worth dying for. At least, I felt this way, and the idea of failing to support Whit, to care for our boys, seemed morally wrong, in spite of the agitated and grasping perpetrators intently advancing the marxist philosophy of a new age.

Ilene and I found a sanctuary of sorts at Mr. Johnnie's, and we liked to go there and talk to Miss Margaret or Mr. William in Shoes, or Miss Jenny upstairs in the Baby Department. I bought a lot of things for Isabel there and they loved us both. Sometimes, if the store wasn't bustling and busy, Mr. Johnnie let me go downstairs to the ancient basement, where there was leftover merchandise clear back to 1900. He let me pick through it to see if there was anything I wanted or needed. He was like that and couldn't do enough for Isabel and me. I liked going in there, hanging around and shopping with Ilene. She was not the shopper that Cynthia was, much more discerning and restrained. She knew what she liked, what she wanted, and in about two seconds, they had a done deal and were wrapping it up with no time wasted on indecision. Generally there was a pattern. We all exhausted ourselves talking about every blessed thing that remotely mattered including the unfortunate hat someone wore to a Bridal Shower last week around the lilly filled pool at Austill on Beauregard Avenue. The main thing was the hat had not come from Mr. Johnnie's millinery department, but from some competitor over in Oxford. Such things were not overlooked, and criticism always followed if a person failed to shop locally. Clothes from Memphis and New Orleans were always recognized right away and the gossip started. Sometimes the clothes even came from New York, but we really hated to criticize those.

When the words finally ran out, Ilene had Amos, the stock boy, go put everything in the car and we went down the street to Estelle's Cafe for pie. She had six kinds, one for every day of the week; coconut cream, cherry, apple, lemon meringue, blueberry and chocolate, except she was closed on Sunday's. There were also pumpkin, pecan and chess pies for the holidays. Her front window had one of those flashing blue neon signs that spelled out "Estelle's," and inside were vinyl booths and chairs and formica tables all in powder blue, her favorite color. At one end was a large gold Jukebox where customers dropped in a quarter and played their favorite songs like, "Do You Know the Way to San Jose," "Sealed With a Kiss," or "Little Green Apples." Estelle ran it with her husband, a good man gone to ruin. Theral Haller was a brittle shell of himself now, not the swaggering basketball player with the boyish good looks, not the burnished member of the Varsity Club, not the boy with the pink carnation in the lapel of his blue sport coat at the Prom, not any of those things. Not anymore, not since the accident, the night that changed a happy world into an ugly one littered with shards of broken glass and blood. He dropped his date, Estelle, off at home after Prom and went out with his drinking buddies to drag race, carouse the county and pick up some good-time girls like Faye and Monica whose favorite pastime was riding around in cars at all hours of the night drinking and smoking and carrying on with a bunch of liquored up boys. A little way out of town, at Fowlers Store, a mean, dark stretch of county road ran straight as an arrow ten miles to a "Y" at Blakes's Crossing. The usual competition was to see who could make the run the fastest. The record was six minutes and thirty-two seconds, set by Willis Palmer last Fall in his 1949 hot rod. Theral and his friends thought he could beat that. So, they all stood around in the headlights passing around beer and liquor until enough talk and bravado rose sufficiently into the night.

 Theral was driving his best friend Duke's brand new 1950 sedan with a monster 303 engine. Monica piled in beside him balancing their bottle of liquor, oohing and ahhing about how he would leave Willis in the dust. Faye climbed in with Willis, downing another beer, laughing and purring in his ear about this being like taking candy from a baby, and both cars peeled out into a black straightaway. Nobody knew how it happened exactly, but around the three mile marker both cars spun off the highway in a crash that drove Willis dead into a tree killing him and his rider, Faye, instantly. Theral flipped and rolled over several times throwing Monica through the windshield and leaving her limp body crumpled in a ditch. He crawled out without a scratch, and they found him later, drunk and in shock, stumbling in the pitch dark down the middle of County Road 15. Everybody said it was just a bad accident, just boys helling around, but three people were dead and the guilt of it ate him alive. All these years later the memory of it still twisted between his shoulder blades like a knife. Estelle forgave him, they had a child and she opened her pie shop, but he never quite shook it, never quite forgave himself. He helped out behind the counter, his even, deliberate movements so measured, as if every slice of pie was a slice of restitution, and his angular face was tan and hardened now and haunted with a worried map of lines that only softened sometimes when he smiled.

—Howdy Miss Isabel, he always said, taking her tiny hand. What kind of pie does your momma want today? Look at you all decked out in your polka dots. One of these days before too long you're going to have our own slice of pie, you know that? That's right, missy. And, I bet your favorite will be cherry, 'cause you're already so sweet.

Theral went on and on trying hard with me, with everybody who sat at that counter. He was kind to everyone but himself, self-sentenced to the penance of an undeserving soul who had to earn the right to be here, daily scratching for his little scraps of happiness. Sometimes as he worked away behind the counters, a catchy tune playing on the Jukebox, I saw him straighten a little, like the world was all fine; a disguise that hovered there for meager seconds, like camouflage. In reality, his crushing burden of regret was not entirely unlike the bank officer's down at the Savings and Loan who had a quiet affair with his secretary until it became messy and his wife divorced him and took the children, or that Mullins man who owned a tire store and managed to kill his own grandchild in a tractor accident. The weight of loss settled on all those men with an intractable permanence that clung to them now. Drowning in regret, they wore it like sackcloth, and everyday's battle was a silent search for reprieve. They weren't alone in this. Some number of the mild and harmless occupants of our town, shoppers and church goers and farmers and housewives, crafted disguises for the thousand things that ate away at them, too, walking around everyday smiling and pretending that the world was all fine.

People in town mostly bought their pies from Estelle's and their cooked vegetables from Sally's over on one of the side streets. Sally's momma had run a boarding house and she cooked all day every day for most of her life after her shiftless husband ran off to California leaving them all destitute. I heard her refer to him more than once as "a worthless piece of ____." Her greens simmered with salt pork were an institution and her fried corn bread, some people called hoe cakes, was legendary. She said the secret was frying them in a whole lot of bacon grease and lard. She did squash and fried okra, mashed potatoes and gravy and fresh corn in season. There was always fried chicken, too, and country ham. Everything was hot in long servers right in her kitchen, and everyone just came in the side door and told her what they wanted. Dinners in many dining rooms around town would have suffered without her to rely on. I know Cynthia sent me down there pretty often to get some of Sally's greens and the corn, "if she's got it."

Back at the farm, we had our own versions of all of that. Peach kept us from destitution, and like Sally, had simmering pots of something on the stove all the time. So, our institutions in Fontaine were not clinical creations with fancy storefronts and impersonal employees. They were the stuff of elbow grease and affection, honest dealing and homegrown self-reliance, made with our own hands to sustain ourselves and our neighbors. The simplicity of it worked, and succeeded for long decades here where the lessons of survival were learned early, learned well and passed on so that all of us could enjoy it now. I dwelt among this small sea of inhabitants who were gifts, living blessings that made everyone's life easier, and a little better than they might be otherwise. Whit would come home, I hoped, to this place where he clearly belonged, eating Estelle's pie and Sally's fried corn bread and walking those fields that led down at dusk to the bottoms. And if only his body came home to us, his last breaths expended on a battlefield, then he would lie here, safe in the same ground with his family, buried next to his grandfather at Fernwood. The old pink roses long planted there at the edges of the plot, waited for him, and I knew he liked that, the certainty of it. I tried hard though, not to dwell on it or even think it. I pictured him living, always living.

CHAPTER EIGHT

JUST PEACHY

The old, widely used colloquial phrase from these parts, "just peachy," meant that everything was just fine, better than fine. And everything was just peachy, until it wasn't. Early in the summer, one day when Isabel and I had gone uptown, suddenly things weren't peachy anymore. I was in Mr. Johnny's sitting downstairs in the front window trying on shoes, Isabel half asleep in her carrier beside me on a maroon velvet chair. I had a black leather pump in my hand just then, sliding it onto my outstretched foot when I looked up and saw his face. He hung up the phone at the front desk, his face ashen and stood frozen just for a moment in the morning light pouring across the sidewalk through his doorway. Walking over to me, he hesitated for one split second before he spoke.

— You need to go home right now.
— Why… what's happened? What's wrong?
— You just need to get back out to the farm, he said again.
— Should I go to Cynthia's?
— No, they're already there.

And that was when I knew something bad had happened.

It was a lot of miles, ten miles of wondering, ten miles of imagining the worst and ten miles of tears that already began to fall. When I pulled into the drive there were cars everywhere, Whitney's and R.J.'s and other cars I didn't recognize. There were strange faces, solemn and quiet on the front porch, and then Cash, R.J.'s boy, told me. They found her, asleep they thought, on her old bench out by the garden. Harlan and Sully, the hired hands came up from the barn to see about barbed wire for the fence Peach wanted them to fix. She was sitting there in her old wide brimmed hat, the one she always wore, leaning against the wild Hackberry tree, a gallon bucket of just picked tomatoes beside her. It turned out that she had passed, been lifted up by the angels into heavenly realms while I was trying on shoes. I couldn't have felt worse. If only I had been here. If only I had stayed to help gather tomatoes and okra this morning instead of stupidly going to town. She said she needed more canning jars and I told her I'd get them at the hardware store while I was in town, but that could have waited. Nothing could or ever would make up for her passing, alone in her garden with that bucket of tomatoes.

Whitney and R. J. were distraught, but forced now to think about a funeral. They were completely unprepared, as if they had expected Peach to be here with us forever. The doctor said that her heart just gave out, that it was her time, but it was a sad and complicated business all the way around and we all were suffocated with grief. Whit would have to be notified. He would have to come home for the funeral, not the homecoming any of us envisioned or hoped for. And he did. He did come home, all the way from South East Asia, and I drove like bat out of hell all the way to Memphis to meet him at the plane. He walked across the tarmac toward me and we collapsed into each others arms weeping like two inconsolable children. Fernwood received another Rutledge soul on Thursday afternoon, the fresh turned earth waiting for Peach to rest beside A. W. Funerals were a blur. Everybody said so. We went through the motions but it didn't seem really real. The reception afterward was at the house. Cynthia and Ilene ramrodded the whole thing with the practiced skill one expects at such times. The neighbors brought cakes and pies and deviled eggs, casseroles and chicken salad that we could "keep in the refrigerator for later." The buffet struggled under the weight of all our family silver trays and cut glass bowls and platters. Side tables were stacked with tall glasses and pitchers of iced tea and fruit punch, and the countryside all came to pay their respects to a neighbor and friend. I can't think of it now without weeping. There would never be enough words to describe her, and what she meant to me. She was probably the closest thing to a real saint that I ever knew.

We all stood around talking that day, as people always do after a funeral, saying the right words that seem appropriate and inadequate. Miss Alma just hugged me for a long minute and said if I ever needed anything, to call her. Then I watched her shoulders slump just a little as she stepped off our front porch and into her car. How many of these things had she been to? How many times had she risen to the moment, offering grace and consolation, and then walked away all alone to her own empty house in a late afternoon with the light slipping away. Estelle came, and Mr. Wade, the Sisters, and Mr. Johnny and Father Ed. And, Whit did hold Isabel for the first time, genuinely thrilled with his little bundle of joy. He would love her, and she would love him as nobody else could, and everything would be alright. Someday, it would get better.

His emergency leave lasted a whole thirty days, days of grief and joy all mixed together, and we sat on the front porch together rocking Isabel as if there was no other moment in the world but this moment.

It became clear at once that I would live in the house alone now, and R. J. would run the place, keeping up with the maintenance and books and taxes. Whit would know that Isabel and I were safe and in only a few more months he would be home. They settled it, the three of them, the plan for the place now, sitting around Peach's dining room table piled with papers and documents and bills. Everything seemed straightforward enough and we began the first days of waking up in Peach's house without her in it. We moved furniture and cleaned and sorted through her things, trying to decide what should go to whom, and that was when I saw finally the real simplicity of the life she lived. I never even paid much attention to her clothes or what she wore, but I was astonished now that she had only about a dozen dresses to her name, all the same dark shapeless garments worn exclusively by the women of her era. Pants were an unknown. I never saw her in anything but a dress, and never, ever saw her wearing makeup. I felt rising within me a great anger toward myself and a deepening regret. I lived with this woman, saw her everyday and never even noticed that we should go shopping for her a new dress. She was the authentic product of her birth in 1896, right at the turn of the century, before the days of bobbed hair and newly unconstructed undergarments. She came of age in the roaring twenties, when city women were cutting there hair, rouging their cheeks and dancing the Charleston in shockingly revealing, short, fringed frocks leaving little to the imagination. The cultural upheaval of those days revealed in women's fashions and loose behavior failed to permeate all of the rural South, and Peach, like her sisters on the farms and in the hollows of the hills, chose the known paths of faith and family and a lifetime of hard work. Her closet was evidence of this, the life she had settled on. And, after all these years, A.W.'s clothes, his Sunday suit and work clothes still hung there in the closet beside hers.

Whit left us too soon. I had gotten used to waking up next to him, talking in the kitchen, making coffee and toast to carry out onto the porch. We sat on faded floral cushions in the dark old wicker chairs, angled to catch the first rays of morning light, watching it come up slow, filtered dim and pale through the pecan grove. From the very first second he came into this world, Peach favored him above all others and always called him, "Sonny Boy." It seemed that we could still hear it sometimes, her voice softly calling out from somewhere. His warmth was like a borrowed gift, and it would leave us soon enough. Isabel and I drove him the long miles to Memphis to catch his plane, saying good-by again, him leaning over the baby in my arms to kiss us good-by. I watched him walk away tall and straight in his flight jacket and the hat with the wings on it, every step taking him farther and farther from us. There was an emptiness when he left. It matched the yawning barrenness of Peach's absence, compounded now by the first beginnings of imagining what life would be like now without them. This business of surviving was going to require grit. I could see that now. And, in many ways, Peach had done her work well, preparing us for it. Those first weeks were mainly going through the motions of living. I wandered around the empty house trying to decide what to change, or whether I should change anything. This house was obviously mine and Whit's now, or it would be when we came back here to live after he finished service. We would wind up probably down at Ft. Wyles near Enterprise in south Alabama, and he would instruct until his discharge. Then we would be here and live here just as Peach and A. W. had done, at least that was one of the possible futures. Or, he might want to fly and that would take us to the far away places of my imagination. But first, before we stepped into the dream of any future, he needed to make it back to us. He had to come home.

In the world outside there were spiritual rumblings across the planet that reached all the way to our cocoon of Fontaine. A thirst for Eastern religions appeared. Rock stars, celebrities and artists, hungry for new found enlightenment went on highly advertised Eastern pilgrimages, traveling with their personal guru's and ascending the rising heights of Kathmandu to Swayambhunath. There, below the Buddhist stupa at the crest, stretched the vast green plains of the Kathmandu Valley, a stirring invitation to meditation and the door to inner peace. From these personal exertions came insights and interior revelations that calmed the repressed depths of the subconscious. At least, that's what they said in the animated interviews afterward on the television talk shows. These excursions, captured in stirring photography, generally reflected processions of seekers in the long, flowing robes typical of holy men ascending the spiraling heights toward spiritual enlightenment. The images of their holy ascent and the power of these new ideas might have been a little oversold by the television journalists breathlessly covering the intriguing panorama of foreign religions. The whole thing seemed pretty out of reach for regular people, especially folks in rural Mississippi, but the aesthetics of the Buddhist monks and Hindu Brahmins swept in on cultural tides across continents and now lapped gently at American shores from Florida to San Diego. Transcendental Meditation leapt to national recognition, anchored and spread by the accompanying fads of Indian music and clothing like the ubiquitous Nehru jacket which suddenly was everywhere. Ultimately, this bold new fashion statement failed to arrive in our little hamlet, as did nascent, foreign divinities lacking the fertile ground necessary to attract adherents.

I thought about the incongruity of all of this, the collision of two such radically separate worlds, and I thought about Peach and what  she would say... Not a lot probably. She went sometimes down to a little clapboard country church pastored by some distant relation of hers. She sat on the long wooden pews of her ancestors and sang the songs of the ages with the stoic fear of God learned from early childhood accounts of The Ten Commandments. The minister was disinclined to pastoral orations, abandoning the rich, animated illustrations, thunderous speech and fluttering arms manufactured now in the pulpits of other congregations. He was a simple man convinced of simple truths, and Peach had been steeped in its splendid simplicity for decades. Her everyday life never failed to reflect that. No foreign deceiver, no newly celebrated pagan deity would ever claim her attention or affection. She had been mercifully inoculated by a lifetime of realities that drew her faith close around her, familiar and sound enough to rely on in the face of every need. That small white church, plain and unadorned, spoke volumes, and the plain and unadorned shepherd of its flock spoke volumes, too. When I sat on those simple pews without her now, it seemed as though she was still here, still occupying that familiar seat, still ready to step out from the church door and comment that we needed to make a lemon meringue pie for Cash at Sunday dinner, or how we needed to decide if that blue floral fabric would do for a quilt.

I took a real long look at all of that green wallpaper. I wondered for about a minute whether to try to change it, but the house simply wouldn't have been the same without it. It belonged here, and it made me think of Peach, as if she wasn't gone at all, but was still here. It was her wall paper, and I wondered sometimes if she was watching over me from above, hoping my decisions were the right ones. I didn't want to let her down, and for reasons not clear to me, I needed her over arching approval even more than God's. So, I decided to never touch that wallpaper. The kitchen was another thing though, its walls now painted a faded beige. It could see it had also been off-white and mustard yellow at some points in its long history. I wondered if I dared to paint it some color new and fresh inviting in more light. It would be my first ever project. But, before I could even think about starting, the outside, her garden, had to be dealt with. The last of the summer vegetables were coming in, tomatoes and squash, okra and snap beans. I wanted to finish it like she would have. I couldn't can or freeze it all, so I made my own pilgrimages to town and gave it away to appreciative friends or donated it to the church for benevolence suppers. Eventually R. J. came out with his tractor and plowed it all under, smoothing over the soil at the last. Grass and weeds took it almost immediately and nature returned it to the original state in which Peach had found it in 1922. How many people were fed in the forty-six years she cultivated and harvested that ground. Hundreds, but now this small piece of earth was at rest, as she was. Her life was measured and marked by planted gardens, milked cows and chicken dinners, by Wedding Ring quilts, gathered pecans and Blue Willow and by the wide, warm-hearted trail of kindness she left behind her. How rich we all were because she had been here with us in this place, on this piece of ground, and we were better people because of it.

SUMMER

...a thousand questions lived in an invisible atmosphere just out of reach, like phantoms... and the pain of disappointment and regret etched in that soldiers face really was buried deep everywhere, in every crevasse of humanity, waiting for someone to see them.

CHAPTER NINE

OUR DREAMS ARE NEVER SMALL

Cash, R.J.'s oldest boy, took a liking to rodeo. Ever since some local men down in Marion County got together to hold the first rodeo in Columbia in 1935, it had thrived in the state. Cash latched onto the idea, the gritty, hard-bitten romance of it, back in 1965 when he was just a sophomore in high school and some Jackson visionaries launched "The Dixie Rodeo" out at the state fairgrounds. Smaller versions sprang up in counties all over, but the biggest show was down in Leake County, "The Rodeo Capitol of Mississippi," at Carthage. Cash even persuaded R. J. to go down there all the way to Carthage to watch the barrel racing, roping and bronc riding last year just after Christmas. He had all the enthusiasm of a young man about to be eighteen, tall and lean from baling hay and cotton, and he fully intended to be involved with rodeo somehow, someway. Dressed up in our boots and cowboy hats and western shirts with the snap buttons, Cash and I went to the nearby rodeos noon and night. We arrived appropriately in his truck and sat enthusiastically in the rough wooden stands cheering for the bronc riders and barrel racers like we belonged there. He wandered around the chutes, talked to the wranglers and looked at their gear and horses. It was like pouring fuel on a fire.

His plan he told me, one afternoon after we got started talking, was to go on over to law school at Oxford and become a lawyer so he could afford the kind of stock he wanted to buy. His manner was warm like Whit's and he was never bothered by hard work. I thought he had the makings of as fine a man as the Rutledge's had ever produced. His younger brother, Walter, was a wide receiver on the football team, played basketball and a mean piano, and thought opera was "cool." He was spunky and bright and Peach and I went down to the ancient school auditorium in town with its wooden folding seats to watch his induction into the National Honor Society. Cash had some of those same qualities, but he had too, an unnatural sort of patience. He dated girls on Saturday nights, studied for his English and History and Algebra tests, and worked the ground with R. J., but still drifted over to sit with me for long hours at the dining room table pouring over figures for horse trailers and farm trucks and feed as if he had nothing else to do in the world. I suspected he was just doing his part, helping me keep loneliness at bay, a suspicion I later confirmed. Whit asked him to check on me and Isabel now and then and "make sure they're alright." I thought too, that he genuinely liked sitting around in Peach's house at the dining table or on the worn sofa in the living room enjoying the unexplainable comfort of just being there.

    Peach left us alright, but somehow we hadn't left her. The specter of her presence was there in every room, her plain, simple face something more than a memory. I dug out the old family albums from the mammoth walnut trunk at the foot of her bed and looked at the pictures of her and A. W. and the boys when they were small, in tight starched collars and slicked back hair. Folks didn't smile much in pictures back then, not like now, when the smiling, perfect images immediately define a persons class and place in this world. Comparing them, I thought that pictures were made mostly now to hang decoratively on the walls of otherwise bare hallways to be approvingly admired as a reinforcement of status, or in offices behind a desk commemorating ones standing and ability to produce appropriate children. These faded and fading images were larger, grander in their own way, the faces undisturbed by the artificial influences that swallowed us up as a people entirely now. I loved looking at them, at the mostly unlined and unmade up faces of the women in their long, severe dresses. They were, in their own way, the guardians of an era. They had lived it and managed it well.

Peach was not a beauty, not in the way people usually think of it. Not like my own grandmother, who for sure was a dark haired beauty, squired about the countryside by boys in phaetons drawn by spirited horses, roans and bays groomed for impressing certain young ladies and pressing them into compromising positions. There was a class of men who were dandies back then; "all hat and no cattle," as they said in Texas, flirtatious men with flashy smiles and rose filled promises bathed in golden shimmers of moonlight. It was not too hard to be captured by the irresistible heat of romance that lead to matrimony now and regret later. This was what happened to my grandmother, and she spent a lifetime paying for it, raising her children practically alone while her husband was off chasing after fast cars and fast women. He drank too much and too often, led down the easy, addictive path of self-amusement in the smokey company of whoever was flush with enough cash to buy today's good time. He never emerged or deviated from his known path, never expressed remorse, only returning for intervals to blame my grandmother for his inclinations.

—It's your fault, Libby, your complainin' all the time, he'd say.

I knew her husband, my grandfather, knew him when he was older and his world had lost all of its shine. He needed us then, needed us to pretend all of those years never even happened. He was back now and everything was supposed to be just fine. Libby was stuck with him now, and because he was down to living on his Social Security, he was only able to be out at the Black Horse drinking with his friends on Friday and Saturday nights. The rest of the time he was forced to plow and plant and try to raise enough food for them to live on. He worked at it with what he had left in him, cutting furrows in rocky Arkansas soil, walking behind Old Boy, their aged brown horse pulling the plow. He raised decent crops of corn that stood tall and green, and a good field of potatoes that we harvested and stored sprinkled with lime in the cool root cellar under the house. I say "we" because I spent summers there growing up and did my share of digging, feeding chickens, gathering eggs and hanging wash out to dry. These were some of the reasons I became a hardened city girl. There was only so much romance in hoeing weeds and chasing snakes out of a hen house.

Peach managed to make the wise choice of waiting to marry and then settling down with A. W., not a flashy man by any standards. "He's a good, hardworking man," her momma said, and back then that was enough. He would farm and feed cows, she would cook and put up vegetables for the winter and when they had saved up enough money they might be able to put on a new roof. There was no thought of new clothes or new cars or any such thing as a vacation, and they lived with the same frugality and determination as their neighbors. Those were really the same qualities still required for life on this place. Although Cash grew up as his true mother's son, at ease with opera and Hudson River School landscapes, he never wavered in his understanding of the land and the sacrifices that went with it. He walked me through his idea; now that Whit and I would live here, we might be partners in the livestock business. We could put pens and new fencing down in the old hay fields of the lower forty, and build a bridge over the old marshy area that flooded because of the beaver dam when the river came up. Then we could get to the old spring with its continuing flow of cold water and make a small reservoir to water the stock. He had it all figured out and I listened and encouraged his dream because I didn't have any good reason not to. The young are often sometimes the victims of the old, or at least their dreams are. I was a believer in dreams myself. Maybe, against the ugly odds of life, dreams were the thing we clung to in the hopelessness of a dark night when sleep deserted us and we questioned whether living had any real purpose at all. So, Cash talked and I listened and we ate frozen pizza on Peach's dining room table among his scattered hand-scrawled notes and numbers, and it was enough right then, enough to make us both happy for a while. It seemed right, one of Peach's grand boys and me, sitting in her house, determined to get on with life like she did. Exactly like she did.

It was an odd existence, living with phantoms, people that seemed to be here, but really weren't. I had a few of those. Peach might still be here in spirit, or maybe she occasionally looked down from above or popped in and out of eternity, however the afterlife works. I wasn't sure. I thought that possibly, when we needed somebody, the Creator knew about it and sent someone down to save us in our moment of crisis. Maybe they had morning meetings up there with heavenly folders listing the most needy, the one nearest the dark ends of despair. I remembered that scripture from Isaiah, "Whom shall I send, and who will go for us? Here am I Lord, send me." A lot of humanity and inhumanity flooded in on the precipitous tides of war. How many souls right now were desperately seeking the same thing, reprieve. Reprieve from the grueling side effects of living. One returned soldier I knew about shared a dorm room at Southern with a jazz nut and a pre-med hopeful. The vet survived on booze and dime bags more or less permanently all semester, his supplier tossing them down to him from the upstairs window of a frat house. Perpetual numbness provided distance from his desperation for reprieve. It meant survival for another day, not unlike my grandfathers escape into the comforting consolations of whiskey. Alcohol did not accuse. Alcohol did not criticize or adjudicate. It merely comforted within expected boundaries, and sometimes, one hoped, that was enough.

One great enemy, and new to me, was callousness, and it was upon me before I even knew what it was. Peach, somehow, never suffered from it. In spite of years of deprivation, she remained untouched by its harsh effects. But, I felt it first when a soldier, the relative of a local man I knew, sat down at the table next to Isabel and me at Estelle's. Sullen and hard, he slumped over the blue formica table and stared down at his coffee and blueberry pie as if they were bitter enemies. On leave between military tours, he was angry and lost in a world he didn't recognize anymore among people who didn't recognize him anymore either. But, Isabel and I were generally harmless and disarming and pretty soon he started talking, like local people always do, as if he couldn't hold back. It took me a few minutes to really grasp what he said, and I thought for one hard second that I really didn't want to hear his story. I didn't want to see him or even listen to him because I just didn't have it in me that day. I was engulfed in struggles of my own.

But, providence stopped me. It came to me that maybe, if this was Whit sitting right here in front of someone, I would beg the gods for them to listen to him, to be kind, to let him lean on them and find rest for just one blessed minute. This isolated and unhappy soldier was somebodies son, someone's brother or father and for whatever reason, their affection for him could not reach him here. He did talk some more and seemed more and more at ease eating Estelle's blueberry pie, and even smiled at Isabel as if he could see maybe, what life could actually be again. He stood up finally, walked over to the cash register to pay his bill and went away in better shape than he came in, comforted and maybe even hopeful, maybe even saved from the demons dogging him that day, eager for their pound of flesh, ready to pounce on a struggling soul hanging on by his last thread.

Lots of folks talked about the Lord's work as if it was something that only happened at church when the organ was playing the beckoning cords of "Just As I Am." But, I wondered how much salvation happened in coffee shops eating blueberry pie. How much compassion flowed in-between the vinyl booths and formica tables that truly sustained and changed lives. What if souls hung in the balance on a Tuesday morning right here in Estelle's Cafe, and we were too blind to see it. Unexpectedly, I was helpfully reminded of the needs of someone other than myself and it felt good, really good. I gathered up Isabel and walked outside into a blue morning. I felt almost as if I'd never seen blue before. It was a heavenly color, and I thought God must really like blue to make so much of it. And, He must like green because there is a lot of that, too. Did we stop seeing not just people, but colors, too? Did deadness and callousness, those shrewd enemies of our souls, overtake us with the subtlety of emerging fog, slow and invincible until we were immersed in it at last, and once its prisoners, unable to escape? The hints of answers to a thousand questions like that lived in an invisible atmosphere just out of reach, like phantoms. And I thought, the pain of disappointment and regret etched in that soldiers face really was buried deep everywhere, in every crevasse of humanity waiting for someone to see them.

Out at the farm, things changed, a shift so slight, that I might have missed it. Something in the universe was different now, and I was different now, too. Myra came up to see me, distraught at my loss, and brought with her gifts of comfort and compassion that I sorely needed. Sometimes, we needed things that we didn't even know we needed, a paradox that added fuel to an already incendiary fire ready at any second to a become a raging inferno. Cumulative grief was still grief, just more of it, and I grieved for those boys that came home now to an unwelcoming and ungrateful world of arrogant, resentful people who were genuinely unworthy of them. They deserved to be met with appreciation for all their sacrifices, but even the Army orders advised returning servicemen to wear civilian clothes and not military uniforms when they arrived in San Francisco. How could this be? I saw the latest installment of the violent protests in Berkley on the news, and I pictured our boys on the receiving end of that. I hoped that Whit, when he returned to us, would fly in through LA. and not San Francisco, and wouldn't be assaulted or taunted. At least the only people who greeted him there, handing out stems of daisies to everyone who walked by were the harmless and obsequious Flower Children, the holdovers from the previous, "Summer of Love," still looking to spread, "Peace, man, Love." He wouldn't be exposed to the Beat Generation out at North Beach or the cool looking acid heads and bohemian hedonists high on LSD and psychedelic musical musings. It was the mother ship of the Hippie Generation, a pitre dish of the counterculture's exotic clothes, long hair and sexual liberation; one hypnotic, drug filled trip laced with the hostile prose of the poster children of the moment. None of us who lived in the non-rarified air of north Mississippi understood it. There was actually a group bent on revolution down in Hattiesburg at Southern Mississippi, and they marched all around campus in their armbands, announcing their arrival to all of creation. Who in the world understood that? One of my friends who was there told me about the whole thing. He said they all couldn't believe it, right here in Mississippi parading around like a bunch of hippies, like it was okay.

Myra brought something valuable with her, friendship, unvarnished and free. It didn't require me to do a single thing except bask in it. Words and explanations were unnecessary, and her presence gave me more hope than I had felt in a long time. We sat out on the porch in the mornings, feeding Isabel her oatmeal and pureed pears out of jars heated in a pan of semi-boiling water until it was sufficiently warmed. Myra loved to feed Isabel, doing the impossible task of keeping baby food from going absolutely everywhere. It really did have migratory qualities. I suspected she enjoyed the convenient concept of "rent-a-baby," where, when you tire of the demanding little thing you can just hand it right back over to its rightful parents and go on your merry way, thanking God that it isn't yours. She did well though, and Isabel wasn't difficult, thankfully, not like the screaming baby belonging to one of my neighbors. She lived in a kind of hellish purgatory with that child, sleeping intermittently and dosing it with paregoric in self defense. I was fortunate to escape that particular sentence of motherhood, Doll Baby being possibly the most agreeable baby ever to arrive in this world. Myra had the good fortune to have extended days of vacation which she saved up and now squandered on me. They weren't wasted and she came to see the quiet of the farm as the haven that it was. She drank wine and napped in the wicker chaise in the afternoons and I went out to the mailbox to see if a letter came. Then I walked back with it, remembering for a moment that Whit's hands touched that paper and his lips actually touched the back flap. I pressed my lips against it too, sometimes, because his lips had been there. I never rushed reading the letters. I wanted to make the moment last. It was so disappointing when I reached the end.

It was the height of summer now, and Myra left me, driving away in her roadster in a puff of dust, her radio on full blast leaving behind her the strains of "Stoned Soul Picnic." It hung in the air mingled with the dust of her departure in a faint haze trapped beneath the pecan trees heavy now with leaves and this years fall crop of Stuarts and Paper-Shell's. I liked picking up pecans, and I especially liked having someone shell them for me. There would be enough for pies and Christmas fruitcakes, and plenty to sell if everything went right. It was hot, but not the suffocating heat of some Mississippi summers when the corn was all burnt brown and the soybeans went all limp and flat in the fields. Enough rain had fallen at just the right time to bring R.J.'s cotton almost to full bloom and this year looked like a very good year. He could take a breath now, probably, and begin to think about how rich they were going to be. I wondered how the old timey people made it, farming in the early days and dependent on the eccentricities of nature, as we were. How had the migrating Cherokee fared in their settlement over in the raw wilderness above Tunica as the eighteenth century closed around them? Were there wild pecans and hickory nuts, wars and rumors of wars then, too? What must that have been like; fighting and foraging, wrestling an existence from the earth? Were their trees just as green, their waters just as cool, their hearts just as full of need as ours right now? Is that what the Immortals were for, such a time as this? Did we have our own Immortals sent down to comfort and console us in invisible realms we could not see?

CHAPTER TEN

A BISCUIT BUTTERED ON BOTH SIDES

I got started drinking hot tea in the mornings out of Peach's Blue Willow china cups. All of the pieces were arranged in her big china cabinet; plates and bowls, cups and saucers, serving platters and pitchers all waiting for the woman who would never come again. They were mine now, apparently. Cynthia and Ilene had their own china and crystal, so now I had Peach's Blue Willow. It was the only thing she ever collected that I knew of, and she carefully bought it a piece at a time over the years. She inherited her grandmother's silver, stored in the buffet by the fireplace. When Whit and I married I chose a china pattern with pheasants and ducks, but I only had a service for six so far. But now, Blue Willow came along, a blue and white porcelain thread that connected me to the past, a history I was part of. I loved the romantic Blue Willow story of the two young lovers who had been forbidden to marry and were then turned into birds by the gods and flew away together. When I looked at those dishes, or touched them, or reached into the china cabinet just as Peach had done, I felt the same pleasure she felt. I never passed the cabinet, groaning under the weight of service for twenty-two, without experiencing a deep attraction to it and feeling her close to me. So, in morning's slanted first light I sat out on the front porch in her wicker chairs, read and drank tea from her Blue

Willow cups. Good china, good tea and a good book seemed like a good fit, and I liked just looking at the tea cup of warm amber liquid and the stack of books on Peach's handmade doilies covering the worn table top, a small vignette that felt just right.

There was a new woman at Ilene's, a bespectacled historian wearing a small gold cross, absolutely devoted to The Fern Society and newly borrowed from some elevated institution to teach a terrifyingly academic seminar at the college. I saw her first reclined against the tobacco colored cushions of Ilene's wicker sofa at ease as if she was born right here in this place and nibbling on a cheese straw. She was a very easy soul to like, and similar in many ways to Father Ed. Like him, she indicated her belief in silence as a virtue, and possessed the kind of calm that made me think she was laboring in these fields for a long time. It turned out that she came by her disposition honestly. Her brother, Thomas, was a Cistercian who took his holy orders and resided now as a contemplative at the sequestered Trappist haven, Assumption Abbey, in the Missouri Ozarks. I never knew anyone personally who became a nun or a priest, and I was very curious about convents and monasteries. What did they do there?

— Well, she said, they worked to support themselves, and gathered seven times a day according to the Liturgy of the Hours. They were beginning to consider the idea of baking fruitcakes as a source of income and mostly lived a silent life of prayer and reflection.

Holiness and silence appealed to me for some reason, probably because of my current life balanced so precipitously on the cliffs of despair. She suggested I read, The Seven Story Mountain by the famed Trappist from The Abbey of Our Lady, who died suddenly and tragically this year. I added it to my growing list of important books to read before I was twenty-five, a kind of pact I made with myself because I feared becoming dull and possibly boring from my semi-isolation at the farm. I sewed Isabel's tiny dresses and mine, fed us, managed Peach's house and stayed busy with Ilene and Cynthia, but I also thought about God and read the sort of books that people read when they thought their spiritual development was limited. If Whit hadn't been away, if daily I was not plagued by a thousand subtle terrors, maybe I wouldn't have had time to think on spiritual questions. But, Whit was away, and I desperately wanted him to come home alive to me and Isabel and Whitney and Cynthia, and R. J. and Ilene. We felt it, all of us. I hoped that my motives weren't wrong, like a bribe. What if I was interested in God now just because I needed something, and then He never entered my thinking again until suddenly I was desperate again. I hoped my true thoughts weren't like that.

Rockets rained down on Bien Hoa the third week of July. Whit wrote me about it, how many died, how many aircraft were lost or damaged, and they were all in high gear getting ready to go back out and retaliate on the enemy. He and his roommate escaped unscathed in a bunker, but their quarters took an almost direct hit. The headquarters and maintenance depot were thankfully saved, but the rockets hit a C-130 aircraft with 75 men on board leaving the country for home, and every one of them died right there on the tarmac. Whit said he watched them loading onto the plane, lined up wearing their travel khaki's and carrying the duffel bags they packed one last time, probably already counting the hours until they landed on American soil. None of them, or the crew, used to flying in harms way, ever expected they would die that day. How many missions had they flown in and out of here on make-shift runways, dodging mortars and rocket fire. Maybe they were praying right then too, to just make it out of here one more time, but this was not their day.

I got another letter from a pilot in Whit's class. A few of the boys were single and needed mail, just some word from the states to read and talk about. They fought loneliness, too. A group of us sent regular letters and care packages of cookies and cake and chewing gum and other things they asked for. They loved those care packages. Wallace, a pilot from California that we wrote to, always shared whatever he got with his team and set the contents out on the bar in the club for everyone to admire for a minute before they all dived in. He wrote me that ghosts of the French soldiers seemed to appear in the dark recesses of the club sometimes, watching a lone figure leaning on the bar, taking his one long, last drink of the night, his shoulders sagging under the weight of todays death. He said he thought their spirits came to join their fellow warriors just to be in their company, the company of men like themselves. I could believe it. Maybe the fallen lingered in a purgatory, waiting for their moment of ascension, still yearning for companionship. The world brimmed with opinions about the other side of the veil, the beyond of inexpressible half light. If there were wandering souls out there, I felt for them. They had their counterparts among the living, the ill-fated souls who passed through the teeming corridors of this life, yet never arrived at home here.

One soldier, Bradley, wrote me how much he loved the Vietnamese children. They all gathered around and he gave them candy bars. Many were orphans, their parents dead in some attack on their village. In a war torn country there was no social safety net, nothing to save them. That they survived at all was a miracle. His folks lived in Tuscaloosa, and they kept him busy with all the news of the latest Crimson Tide games. College football was a great consolation to every soldier I knew, and they loved to hear about baseball and basketball, too. I tried to keep up with the games so I'd have something to write about. If Arkansas beat Texas, some people were happy and yelling "Woo pig, Sooie." If Alabama won over Georgia, the streets would be full of cars honking horns while everybody shouted "Roll Tide." Our boys over there were missing that, and we tried to make them feel a part of it anyway. Fall was coming up, and pretty soon there would be real games to go to. Whitney and Cynthia never missed an Ole Miss game. She was a cheerleader back in the day and never lost her school spirit. Whitney just liked to watch the game and catch up with all their old friends and tailgate at The Grove. R. J. couldn't drag Ilene to a ball game so he loaded up a carload of men and off they went to Mississippi State to ring those noisy cowbells. He loved it and tried to hide the disappointment of Cash wanting to go to Ole Miss. Football in the South, it was the true religion.

Peach's dining room table seemed littered almost permanently now with Cash's notes and Whit's and other soldiers letters, the ones just received and the ones overdue for answers. I sat there among them, the words of these boys, at night now, their hopes and dreams all spread out before me like a tapestry of wants. I read their letters slowly and I thought about what I would say if we were having an actual conversation. Bradley wanted to have an auto dealership in Tuscaloosa and live on Cherry Street right near his folks. He loved cars, and I sent him ads torn from the local paper showing pictures of the newest models. Charlie was one of life's forlorn survivors with little family, hanging on so tight to whatever little dreams he managed to make all by himself. Dave had business plans, accounting and finance, maybe insurance thrown in for good measure. He'd like to have his own agency in New Orleans. He loved New Orleans and wanted to live up town on St. Charles or some street like that. The sounds of the street cars encompassing the sedate, oak lined blocks near the river were his idea of heaven. It was easy to agree with him. I loved New Orleans, too. It was one of my favorite places on earth; the sprawling enthusiasm of Canal Street, the food and bluesy libations of the French Quarter. Dave's ideas were pretty good.

I wandered around Peach's house daily now and felt less and less like an interloper or a surreptitious snoop, peering into cabinets and drawers that were none of my business. Her pantry was quite a thing, the spacious shelves rose to ceiling height stacked with neat rows of jars canned with the bounty of Peach's garden. Her pale floral recipe box of handwritten cards, stained and grown brown now, sat on one shelf, faded and splashed with the evidence of their long relationship to her kitchen bowls and spoons. I thumbed through them, thinking how long ago some of these must have been written. They laid there on the counter all those years of cold winter mornings at four a.m. when she cooked up breakfast for A. W. and the farm hands, making biscuits and coffee and eggs and ham and grits that sustained them until lunch, when she did it all over again. Some recipes had little hand written notes on the edges identifying their origins; "Louise Moore's pound cake that she served last Thursday"…or, "Betty Richards says this came from Reverend Potter's wife over in Tupelo"…or, "Good, moist cake, use Pet milk and extra chocolate"…or, "This was good for lunch with sliced ham and pineapple salad."

    I put my own growing box of recipes and notes and lists of figures on the shelf beside her recipe box. This was my history now, going in beside hers. She canned and froze everything. That corn in the freezer all wrapped in butcher paper was the result of three entire afternoons of work. Peach and I set up work tables, blanched the ears in boiling pots and then cooled them in ice water before sealing them up in white butcher paper for their long nap until winter came and we would really appreciate having them. I looked at all of the jars; the perfect peach halves turned just so the round parts faced out, the potatoes, green beans and squash, the blackberry jam, the okra and tomatoes. Lord, those tomatoes. I helped her with some of those, doing the part I hated most, blanching and peeling them. The skins were supposed to just come right off, but I never had the knack for it. I'm sure she just shook her head, up to her elbows in deteriorating tomatoes and thought quietly how useless young people were. What was I going to do with all that food? It would last a year for sure, maybe even two, but after that somebody would have to throw it out, all that work wasted. I felt like we should start using it up, and then start giving it away. We needed to begin having Sunday dinners, or Saturday dinners or lunches or whatever it would take to get everyone here in Peach's dining room again.

Sunday afternoon dinner, that lynchpin of Southern domesticity, rendered a happiness we all crucially needed whether we knew it or not. It was a universally understood truth, one desperately missed now that Peach was gone. I could not stop thinking about succulent roasts and fried chicken all golden right out of hot grease, and I began to feel a deep longing for it; for Blue Willow plates heavy and overfilled, dripping with gravy and purple hull peas and stewed okra, while all of us sat around the table eating and talking as we had done for years and years. What if we all just started doing that again, having those dinners whenever we could? Those perfect jars of fruits and vegetables, canned with love by Peach, deserved their place on the Rutledge table. And, that corn was special. One bite and you knew it. Peach did all of it to feed her people. So, I mentioned the idea to Cash when he was over one afternoon to talk his usual talk about horses and saddles and rodeo, and then to Ilene, and I talked to Cynthia last because I knew how little she cared about eating canned vegetables on Blue Willow out at the farm. But, she surprised me. She agreed and thought it was actually a good idea.

We had our first dinner when the cotton was high and bloomed out into squares and R. J. was in a fine mood, and Cynthia, God bless her, was feeling righteous and full of good will. She rose to the occasion with a spectacular amount of grace, as if she were a benefactress bestowing royal largess on her subjects. She brought her famous spoon bread, and a decadent shrimp and crab casserole loaded with heavy cream and gruyere, topped with bread crumbs that came from New Orleans. I wondered how many cows it took to produce that all that cream. The recipe came out of a cookbook from the Women's Association over in Jackson, which was a kind of holy grail for recipes that newly reflected cuisine with style. Anyway, she actually helped set the table and got out the right napkins for us to use, like a regular person. Ilene insisted on contributing pot roast besides her creamed onions and two pies. She brought along a couple of her lonely academics to join us, the pleasant contemplative and a lapsed Christian. Whitney invited two distant cousins from the next county over who "needed family," to join us, so we had a full house. I piled the fried chicken up high on two large platters just as Peach did and cooked up three large jars of green beans, three jars of squash and three big packages of frozen corn on the cob. Mashed potatoes and gravy filled two other large Blue Willow bowls, and I piled up Peach's brown crock with my grandmother's homemade biscuits, which I knew how to make with my eyes closed.

The biscuits were the one of the main things that made me so intent on doing this dinner. Peach made biscuits almost every morning, and Isabel and I sat there in her warm kitchen dissolving in the biscuit ether and watching the butter melt. It was very satisfying.

— Make sure you butter that biscuit on both sides, she always said.

Her strict buttering method virtually guaranteed that each biscuit half was oozing with equal amounts of butter. Her biscuit philosophy was a metaphor for life, of sorts. She believed a well made biscuit deserved to be treated with the deference it deserved, the careful and reverential spreading butter on both of the split halves, not just sticking an indecent hole in it and desecrating the perfect round sides with irregular hunks of butter willy nilly. It was a disservice to the biscuit. Walter forgot this one morning and actually thrust a forkful of butter into the soft edge of a golden biscuit heaving with warmth right out of the oven. She just sighed and looked at him.

— Walter, you're abusing that biscuit.

So, following her good example, I wanted the biscuit of my own life to be buttered well, and on both sides.

Our dinner was a great success, and maybe it helped us all to be together again. We stayed a long time at the table and Whitney had the foresight to set us all up for homemade ice cream. He stayed busy adding salt and ice and turning it until it was just right and then we served it up on top of Ilene's peach pies. We were, in a way, on uncharted ground, this first dinner without our living Peach, and the pie and ice cream felt good, felt right. It was good way to start. There was a mountain of dishes, but we got a sort of assembly line going and made it seem like fun, and for the first time I noticed the chill that usually arrived with Cynthia wasn't there. She left it at home with its unhappy companions and simply drove away without them, and we were all the better for it. It was a good day. Everybody said so.

CHAPTER ELEVEN

THOSE WITH POWER OVER US

Cynthia and I followed all of the latest fashion trends featured on the covers of the latest magazines, and we decided that I needed a fresh, updated look, a new haircut. Guy's on Second was the obvious choice, so I called Miss Edie and set myself up an appointment with Guy himself for Wednesday morning at eleven o'clock. His salon was no sudsy beauty shop, and unlike the others in town, had the only male hair stylist in all of Fontaine County. Typically the exclusive domains of effusive, chatty women, perms and standing appointments, his shop reflected a different direction entirely. For one, it was a large Victorian home complete with a wraparound porch dripping in Boston ferns and pink bougainvillea. He grew up in this house and lived there with his doting mother that he, and everyone else, called Mother Eustis. He was a dutiful son, so much so that the locals suspected his days on this earth would be confined entirely to picnic outings with Mother Eustis in the riverside park, arranging her blankets and adjusting her parasol against the formidable rays of mid-morning. She was delicate and retiring and needed someone to rely on after her unfortunate marriage to a man who fancied cards and gambling more than he fancied her. And Guy, who was born after the wily devil slipped the bonds of marriage, heading downstream before dawn on a Mississippi Riverboat bound for New Orleans, never knew his father or even laid eyes on him his entire life. So, everybody thought Guy's future was on a one-way shaded street holding tea cups for his mother.

They were shocked one day to wake up and find that Guy had bolted, leaving his frail mother behind and fled, apparently, to New York. It caused quite a stir and Mother Eustis received plenty of sympathy until everyone found out that it was her idea. She was craftier than anyone imagined and sturdier, too, now fetching her own tea cups and pouring her own tea and watering her own dripping ferns on the wrap-around front porch. She was seen in the mornings moving about amid the greenery, sitting at her wicker table and drinking tea without needing any assistance with her shawl, and even carrying her own basket of knitting. Apparently immune to the torrent of gossip raging about her, she just smiled and said that Guy had, "gone off to school." Well, nobody believed that. There were speculations, suspicions, innuendos. One version of his disappearance, much talked about at Estelle's, was that he was off living a decadent, bohemian life in the New Orleans French Quarter or worse, among the debauched heathen of San Francisco.

It was quite a shock one day to find Guy returned and his mother actually seen picking him up at the train station downtown in their ancient car. So, the prodigal had returned, at least it seemed so, and Fontaine prepared for the worst, the fusillade of rumors poised to be spread far and wide by the well-meaning and not so well-meaning.

— He's back here. He came in on the train. Have you heard that he's moved right back in with his mother?

They were even more shocked to find out that three days later, another person arrived down at the train station and was seen being picked up by Guy and Mother Eustis in their ancient car; a woman, petite and blond and carrying luggage, a lot of luggage. They even had to have some of it sent by delivery truck out to the house. Folks eventually discovered that her name was Edie, that Guy met her in the Dry Goods Department of Harrod's Department Store in London, married her two years ago, and now had come home with his bride to live with Mother Eustis in their gracious Victorian home on Second Street.

There was more. Guy actually was at a school of sorts. Because of his inclination toward beauty and refinement, Mother Eustis encouraged him to become a hair stylist. He started out apprenticing in New York and then got himself over to Paris to learn from the emerging new darling of the salon world, René-Louis, working in "The City of Light" in a chic salon on rue Notre Dames des Victories. René-Louis made himself famous by his associations with film industry celebrities and their signature haircuts. Guy and others benefited from these useful connections, establishing themselves in the high end, avant-garde salons that now offered Bob's and Flips, Bouffants and French Twists to style conscious women from Europe to New York. Well, Guy finally had enough of life on the continent and decided he and Edie would come home to Fontaine and open a really fine salon catering to the needs of affluent local ladies who otherwise went to stylists in Memphis or New Orleans. Mother Eustis again proved to be a surprising asset, lent them the entire, spacious downstairs of the house for the salon, and moved lock, stock and barrel to the second floor without batting an eye.

So, Guy's on Second was born, and although it shocked and annoyed the other beauty shops in town who clung to permed hair, big rollers, colorful gossip and forty-five minutes under the hair dryer, there was little they could do except complain that a man cutting hair was somehow "unnatural." Some men, in no uncertain terms, even forbade their wives from going to Guy's, but eventually, little by little, women began to apologetically sneak over to him. Guilt lingered a while but pretty soon, seduced by his elegant furniture and cosmopolitan atmosphere, they came over in droves. He gave everybody the celebrity treatment and incredible haircuts, and now women said what everyone thought out loud.

— I'd never go anywhere but Guy's.

So, that's how I came to be in Guy's salon, sitting in his plush, black velvet Louis Quinze style chair, sipping champagne, with the delicate tones of Edith Piaf warbling faintly in the background while a clinician massaged my manicured hands with Panier Des Sens. No, like his other devoted clientele, I would never even think of going anywhere else.

In our town, certain conventions dictated the flow of life with the regularity of planets revolving around the sun. Included in this predictable rhythm lay the happy opportunities for social advancement found in causes, clubs and committees. The civic and social guardians of Fontaine ruled their domains with the fierce determination of a Montana rancher, and everybody knew exactly who belonged where. Each garden club, church committee and social group functioned under the benevolent gaze of its commanding general, or generals, if the person in charge felt like sharing the limelight. These were citadels of public good, usually ruled by battle hardened matrons who guarded their positions with the same internecine spirit seen in the bloody and unfortunate days of the French Revolution. To refer to the French Revolution as "unfortunate"" was a perfect example of the verbal prison our small hamlet embraced without hesitation. Our reluctance to offend rendered us complicit in every form of evasion. Instead of commenting that some well-regarded gentleman had one too many cocktails rendering him unable to find his car, we might blame an interaction with "that new medication." Certain faux pas, however, were unforgivable, and one blunder or near blunder could mean "La Guillotine" and banishment to a social wasteland. Oralee Davenport once wore white shoes to an October picnic in 1957 well after Labor Day, and some ladies still talked about it. They felt that it was the real reason behind her eviction from Tuesday Afternoon Bridge Club. Even woodwork painted the wrong color or a non-pedigreed pastoral picture over the living room sofa lead to eventual and regrettable excommunication by the reigning social arbiters.

At a charity dinner one night, I sat, unfortunately, at the same table with one such person, the loquacious and frilly Miss Etta Banks Eastin. Everyone referred to her as Etta Banks, and after pausing long enough in the decorated entry doors for the appropriate amount of recognition, she descended upon us, her frothy arms dramatically waving like a diaphanous butterfly looking for a place to land. She wore a gossamer cerulean blouse with a pussy bow and a string of pearls, a harmless costume meant to disarm her victims, rendering them more easily bent to her will, an acquired skill, a consequence of being an only child. I think I was the first to feel it, the slow sense of trepidation as it began its gentle, preordained rise at our table, and before she was even seated I wanted to flee. Dinner would soon be ordered all around, and I was already feeling like a warm Hors d'oeuvre ready to be offered up. Odd, I thought, or had thought various times, how typically food and its human companions were consumed at exactly the same time, some morsels being more desirable than others.

Etta Banks looked at me in that appraising way people do when they are putting you firmly in your place. Then settling into her seat, she took up her napkin and took charge, directing the conversation with the fierce authority usually found in conductors of the Philharmonic. I half expected her to whip out her black wand and rap me on the knuckles if I drifted. The first round of white wine arrived just in time and slowly released its pleasing liquid sedation, enveloping us all in a warm dullness that could be a mercy sometimes and still leave a person capable of responding to elementary questions with simple answers like yes and no. This was the safe path. Then the appetizers came, and more alcohol which caused the conversation to lag, so Etta Banks became even more animated. These were the moments she was born for. She was relentless. She regaled us with amusing anecdotes of her Uncle Edward then vacationing in the Berkshires and the time she danced Agamemnon at Jacob's Pillow. Her favorite relative, Aunt Hillis, forsook her elaborate Jekyll Island garden for an entire weekend to be in the audience. Really, Etta Banks was way too much, but any failure to respond positively meant a black mark in her book, and most folks would rather avoid that. I already had two marks against me that I knew about, and I was pretty sure she would see to it that I didn't get invited into the Junior Auxiliary.

There were another couple of ladies that I had the opportunity to observe from time to time, the twins, Mary Margaret and Anna Catherine. Only slightly older than I was, they had both managed to already be married and divorced twice and were seriously looking for number three. Their motto might have been, "Marry often, and marry well." Their daddy, Mr. George, owned a big auto dealership, so they were flush with new cars and new cash. I watched them at the country club, oozing charm all over the available men and marveled at their ability to command adoration without any apparent effort. Men were just hypnotically drawn to them, pouncing like ducks on a June bug. The twins mastered this breathless way of talking, leaning intimately onto a man's shoulder, their eyes glued to his as if in worship of whatever it was he was mumbling about right then. This always achieved the desired effect, securing his immediate and undivided attention. Men fell all over themselves, and it was very educational to watch. They had been doing this for as long as they could remember, probably since first grade, making easy conquests out on the playground even before lunch, and they cut quite a wide swath over at Ole Miss where they were sorority legacies. How many little boys went home to their momma's crying over Mary Margaret or Anna Catherine, and how many mothers had to break the sad news to their boys that sometimes we love people but they don't love us back, and that's the way life is. These girls, now women, possessed qualities I could only dream of, and I was a little envious actually, wondering if I could cultivate some of this for myself. I'll bet the words rapturously falling from their honied lips into the willing ears of men had nothing to do with literature. I mentioned this to Whit, and he brushed it off casually, saying that they were, in his words, "flighty."

Their own mother, sensing danger, wisely suggested they go off to Sophie Newcomb down in New Orleans where they would be safe from the enticements of their favorite hobby, collecting as long a string of admirers as possible. But, they pitched a holy fit and got their daddy, George, on their side and that was that. He sent his girls off to Oxford in a brand new 1958 Convertible, Ermine White and a powder blue interior with a 392 V8 engine, probably to ensure fast trips home on the week-ends so their mother could do their laundry. By the end of their Sophomore year they were both engaged to nice boys with good families from the Delta. They had a double wedding in the gaudy ballroom of the Peach Tree Hotel up in Memphis, and it was all love and kisses until the couples lost their enthusiasm for each other about a year later, and then they went quietly back up to Memphis without quite as much fanfare so family lawyers could discretely handle their divorces. I secretly admired the way they managed it all without seeming tacky. Divorce was rarely spoken of in our world, and then it was whispered about in the hushed tones associated with unspeakable sin. Normally it was the kiss of death. Reputations lay in tatters and families were branded with a lifetime of stigma.

— You remember the Jackson's don't you? You know, those people who got divorced.

But, the twins acted like it was just nothing, and eventually their dismissive attitude rubbed off on everybody until somehow it was alright because it was just Mary Margaret and Anna Catherine being themselves. They fully planned to go on being themselves and never gave two hoots whether people liked it or not, so people shrugged their shoulders and said,

— Oh, that's just the way George's girls are.

Maybe that was one of the things men found so appealing, the unvarnished daring of it. There weren't many women around like that.

Meanwhile back at the farm, I had mail in the box when I pulled up, two letters from Whit and one from Dave. Isabel was over with Cynthia for the day and the house was silent inside and still like houses are when the person who lived there had gone away. I got a cold glass of iced tea, parked myself on the porch in Whit's chair, the one he liked, and slowly read the pages, making them last. Part of Whit's latest letter read, "The last week has been real busy. Got mortared while I was sitting on the strip at Bu Dop. Had hydraulic trouble at Song Be (eight miles north of Bu Dop) and spent most of the night getting it fixed. Finally pulled off about 10:15 and then got mortared again at 10:45. Whew! We got sniper fire here at Bien Hoa (about a mile from our barracks) the other night. Nobody hurt. Tell mom and dad I love and miss them, and hug our baby girl for me...... I got your package yesterday. Thanks for the pillows. They'll be great in my room. Getting sort of hungry now, so I'll go eat over at the mess hall. I believe they've got spaghetti tonight... that's not bad. Love, Whit."

It was a little bit lonely here at the house sometimes in the afternoons while Doll Baby was napping. Peach and I used to sit together, sew on her old Singer sewing machine and watch soap operas on TV..." Peach got a little carried away by the trashy behavior of some of the characters; the seething passions between Miranda, an athletic young nurse who had her eye on the hunky Doctor Rob, with the steel blue eyes and muscular torso. Pretty soon, after a few interludes in his tiny office, he was putty in her hands and they were off for a steamy, week-end fling in Saint Croix that had nothing to do with fishing. It was riveting stuff. In another story, the childlike and innocent Roxanne lay pale and cold, near death at the hands of a seedy hitman hired by a crooked banker trying to hide his embezzlement of her family fortune. Would she be saved? And, who knew about Rachel's illegitimately conceived child? What if Lawrence or his interfering mother found out? Peach and I were pretty immersed in the imaginary struggles of these other people, these actors who filled the screen every afternoon with drama and lust. After some new impending catastrophe, Peach got on the phone with one of her cousins and they talked about the tragedy as if these characters were real. Her comments always reflected her deep disappointment in their behavior.

—I just don't understand how Rachel could treat him like that...She is just going to be the ruin of that boy's life.

Then Peach nodded while her cousin said something along the same lines, and this went on for five or ten minutes until one of them had to, "go get supper on." This was what passed for usual and we all appeared to be real happy to just go right on doing it. It was odd, the things that bound people together. In the right circumstances, even a soap opera could do it.

Folks always said that misery loved company and that was true enough, but the time we spent together had other uses, too. Under what other circumstances would I be here with Peach, or become a grown-up pen pal to boys far away, semi-friends searching for consolation, something in common, something to talk about, something that seemed normal in a world where normal was hard to define. It seemed like we all entered a kind of invisible pact with each other where we didn't much dwell on the bad around us. We looked for the common things to hold onto, little distractions with enough goodness in them to help us all make it through another day. I had new pen pal to add to my list, a Green Beret. He was the very squared away older brother of my high school friend, Ruth Ellen. I knew him slightly from sleep-overs and parties at her house, where we all stood around and played the latest songs on her record player as he watched from an amused distance like a typical big brother. She called me from Atlanta begging us all to write letters to Hardy, so we all did. He found a home on Peach's dining table now with Bradley, Charlie and Dave, boys who needed our attention now. One thing I did know, other dining tables in other homes all over town were covered with the same things; hopeful handwritten notes and care packages exactly like mine, addressed to our boys, full of cookies and candy and pictures, our small way of reminding them that they were loved and missed. Evidence of a world of caring lay scattered on those mahogany and maple and oak surfaces, untidy with remnants of heavy brown paper and thick string and tape. They just stayed there now because everyday, it made us think of them.

CHAPTER TWELVE

THE HARDWARE MAN

T he languid last days of summer overtook us, the ground permanently warm now, and the trees heavy and bent under the heat of August. It was hot everywhere, especially for the student movement. Thousands of them descended on the streets of Chicago for the Democratic National Convention to protest the war, and everything else. Four days and nights of violence spilled out from Grant Park to the International Amphitheater that was ringed with barbed wire and then all the way down Michigan Avenue. In front of the hotel, the Illinois National Guard fired tear gas into the crowd and the Chicago Police clashed with the demonstrators, beating back the advancing protesters with clubs and rifle butts in a smoke filled scene that went on and on for nearly twenty minutes. We watched it all unfold on TV, the Yippies and the hippies shouting obscenities, taunting the "pigs," and parading around an actual pig, "Pigasus," as their presidential candidate. The whole Police Department was down there, plus units of the Illinois National Guard, a total of over 20,000 officers and Guard, according to the TV commentator. Hundreds were arrested and it was hard to have much sympathy now for the surging anti-war crowds as if they were just a bunch of disgruntled and idealistic college kids. The demonstrators poured down Michigan Avenue in violent waves, the incendiary sprawl filtering through the city blocks around the Amphitheater, and the images from that night really changed everything. It was more than just another war protest. America really saw, maybe for the first time, the anti-war mobs marching and shouting obscenities as a revolutionary movement bent on obliterating everything in this country we loved. It was a frontal assault on American goodness, values and ideals. We didn't like it, and we said so. A disturbing litany of upheaval now seemed to hold our entire culture captive from coast to coast in a malevolent death grip. All over Fontaine, at the Rebel Dip, in Wells Department Store and Estelle's Cafe people talked about it. We'd all had enough.

I didn't have Peach to watch the nightly news with anymore. Sometimes I took Isabel and we spent the night in town where I watched TV with Cynthia and Whitney and heard his colorful comments on the spectacle we were witnessing. He had a gift for cool, astute appraisal, and people usually turned out to be exactly what he thought they were. Whenever Doll Baby and I came home again, the house felt a little forlorn, as if it had been deserted and was waiting for someone who loved it to return. Can a house feel abandoned? I thought so. I felt it all the way through me, clear down to my toes. Did the angry young people on TV have any such thoughts about home? Where were their parents? Didn't they have grandparents somewhere, and houses with porch swings and potted geraniums by the front door? Somewhere within them, wasn't there a yearning for family dinners and someone's fried apple pies and children laughing, playing outside on a rope swing? How could they have chosen the hostile, smoke-filled, urban streets over all of that?

I didn't know any young anti-war people personally. I was never closer to any of them than our television set, but the student movement taking America and Europe by storm had clearly embarked on the path of "Carpe Diem." They seized the streets of Paris, Prague and demonstrations closed down The University of Madrid for over a month. The same conflicts followed in Britain at Oxford and Cambridge, the students breaking through police lines there and attempting to overturn the car of an official of the Defense Department. There were sit-ins in Poland, and in Tokyo, the railway station descended into chaos while other student factions filled the streets, preventing former President Eisenhower's plane from even landing there on an official visit. The thing that clearly drove them, their overpowering thirst for change, the combustible fuel of their own passions for liberation of all kinds, never reached into my soul with that kind of tenacity. Perhaps it was stopped at my own borders, the ones I recognized and lived within, the ones marked with invisible signs.

In Charlie's latest letter he mentioned the long missions they were flying lately, and that the V. C. were moving all their heavy stuff, tanks, artillery, anti-aircraft in now, so his unit was busy trying to knock holes in their supply route south of Da Nang. He thought they made a strategic mistake dividing their forces, but he had flown without a day off for over two weeks. Charlie, with his soft ways and diffident manner, reminded me of a boy I knew in high school, just his facial expressions that sometimes seemed so telling. I remembered Vince vividly. He was new to our school, looking hard for friends, and he surprised me one day out in front of the band hall. His folks had just pulled up and he wanted to introduce me to his mother. In almost the same breath, he asked me to go with him to a dance, so I got a good look at his mother's face and her pleading look, begging me to be kind, to say yes. Hers was a face worn with twenty years of wanting things she never got, and now she wanted things for her boy, just a little kindness. I couldn't go to the dance with Vince because I already had a date, but I was cordial about it, smiling and leaning in toward his mother in the passenger window.

—It is so nice to meet you, and how sweet of Vince to ask me to the dance. I'm sorry that I can't go.

—Vince has talked about you, she said, her pale blue eyes searching mine. It is nice meeting you, too.

Then I saw her husband, bending forward to look out at us over the steering wheel and I recognized it; the puffed up face, fat with the self importance of a failed small-town politician, brusque and pushy, desperate for an audience somewhere glad-handing a crowd. His wife was a mere accessory to his existence, possibly in the same category as lawn mower, but requiring even less maintenance.

Success had eluded this man and now, his good looking son was useful only as a means of attracting attention to himself, his achievements mere opportunities to bolster his own standing, or lack of it. He was probably not a reprobate, but he was something even worse, a man who stole souls and drained them of life, leaving them utterly diminished before discarding them as if they were nothing at all. It was obvious what this woman had been through and was still bravely enduring, and she was still trying with everything in her to make a better life for her boy. I wouldn't forget the brave look on her worn face as their aged station wagon slowly pulled away and my little wave good-by to her. I stood there on the curb in my pink dress, caught up in the warm perfection of a Spring afternoon and pictured her as a young girl just like me once, hopeful and full of life, waiting, wanting someone to love her. Instead, she became attached to a man who found her merely useful. There was a world of women out there like that. They just sort of got used up over the years, an almost invisible lifetime of being unappreciated and taken for granted, never really noticed by anyone, not even family, until their funerals. They were briefly and tearfully mourned and then summarily buried, along with all their unrealized dreams and girlish hopes, by people who never really knew them or saw them at all. I did know that look. I saw hints of it in Margaret Allen, and on the face of that soldier I saw in Estelle's. Men got used up, too. There were no "recovery groups" for used people. They just made out the best they could, existing in a threadbare world of self imposed silence and suffering, wishing daily for a way out of their life of misery.

There were occasional offenders in our town, men displaying varying degrees of selfishness. A few were church leaders of varying sorts who casually drifted between polar extremes, leaving behind them trails of invisible carnage. On any Sunday, one particular man I knew was always seen in his impeccable suit, carrying his large Bible, walking the church halls on his way to teach a Sunday School class, the apparent epitome of holiness. His real life was less admirable. His family lived everyday under the harsh and unforgiving lash of criticism. He never missed an opportunity to humiliate his children or embarrass his wife in public, to make them seem small and stupid. It was his mission in life. They all deferred to him, as their souls shrank and became smaller and smaller and even praised him as a "good father" because to say otherwise would make the family look bad. I knew one day in the not too distant future, a funeral would mark his passing. The minister would stand up in front of the grieving family and friends and recite, in typical fashion, the life achievements that were designed to make the deceased a great deal better than he actually was, making him sound like a paragon of virtue because of his long years of commitment to "his faith." I witnessed the everyday reality occasionally; watched his children struggle, timidly advancing one hesitant step at a time, always in fear of being crushed or ridiculed, the bleakness of life settling around them like a dark blanket. They were defenseless, and the wife, terrified of any misstep, had the horrendous job of monitoring every interaction because, "We don't want to upset your father." It was a tedious and debilitating business, and after he was gone, it would take a lifetime of undoing. I wondered if there was any spark of hope that might save them, and the injustice of their misfortune was a grief that never left me. We were all forced to collectively engage in this insidious façade wrapped up in church clothes, disguising evil as good for the mere sake of appearances. How much invisible, possibly permanent, damage was done everyday to innocent souls whose lifetime of personal struggles never ended because of the unrelenting burden of circumstances just like that.

I mentioned this to R. J. as we rode around the countryside in his pickup, the sheer contradiction in plain sight. How could a man like this, from our very own church, be two completely different things; one person at church, and another person the rest of the time? He just said in his relaxed and disarming way that there were a couple reasons for this, like it wasn't the first time the question had been raised.

—Some men were just jerks by nature and no amount of religion was going to change that, he said.

I really felt, strongly, that he wanted to say they were, "pieces of _____," like Sally, but he didn't want to appear coarse and ungentlemanly. There was a second reason.

— These men were now saved, born again. And, our church believed once saved, always saved.

— So now, no matter what they did, they would go to heaven? I said.

— Yes, and all of the folks sitting in those pews every Sunday take a lot of comfort in that.

I had to admit they seemed perfectly happy, as they had been for decades and their parents had been for decades, with the arrangement. Looking through my personal lens, as an uninitiated outsider, there was a certain comforting continuity in the way they carried the burden of their salvation, the main evidence of their redemption being the guilt they were always fretting about, "not doing enough for the Lord," but I could see now why they could rest easy, knowing that their salvation had been secured and recorded on the church rolls. I asked him if all it took to make it into heaven was a church membership card and he laughed and said some folks thought so, not just our church, but other denominations, too. Just believe or be baptized and your eternity was secured. I wondered if possibly there might be more to it than that, and I mentioned to R. J. my misgivings about Sunday School. Why, I asked R. J. was this unpleasant man that I had to chat with every blessed Sunday, who was so vile to his wife and children, allowed to teach anything, let alone Sunday school. He sighed a tolerant sigh and adopted the tone generally used when talking to children.

—We have to accommodate the people who come here, he said. This man's financial support payed salaries and kept the lights on.

Well, that explained it. I wouldn't have hurt R.J.'s feelings for the world, but I decided after Whit came home, I'd really like for us to go somewhere else.

I always looked for ways to encourage Hardy, the Green Beret, and told him funny stories about how I was now running my own covert op and had become the shadowy currier of libations for Cynthia and me, the clandestine bottles of wine we drank while we watched old movies on TV at night. The only liquor store was way out on the edge of town, which made it easier for all the religious people to buy alcohol without being seen. So, she sent me out like a spy, undercover, usually just at dusk where I could more easily escape detection. Then I pulled around to the hidden window in the back where Eldridge, the hulking owner pretended he didn't know me and handed out our illicit bottles of wine through the car window. He went through the same routine for every furtive customer in town, and we all timed our arrivals to avoid the embarrassment of encountering each other. Nobody wanted that. Cynthia felt that people would talk if they knew we were knocking back glasses of wine at night, so we hid the empty bottles in benign paper bags, or sometimes she made me take them away to discard at the farm. Trash men were known to talk, so you couldn't be too careful. One of them saw empty bourbon bottles in the trash can of a local widow and word got out. All it took was one whispered comment like, "You know, she drinks," to ruin a reputation.

The phone rang out at the farm one morning early. It was my uncle, my favorite uncle, Henry. Here was a man that I adored for a lot of reasons, but the main one was that he was just a good man through and through. He spent his whole life among tools, nails, plumbing fixtures, paint, window and door parts and farm implements. He had a hardware store in north Arkansas, and I knew that store like the back of my hand. I loved that unmistakable smell of hardware and chicken feed. He was indispensable. People came in and asked him how to fix any and everything. He had parts back in the stockroom for just about any appliance ever invented. More than one man loaded up his mower and brought it down so Henry could "have a look at it." He spent long days on his feet helping customers, talking to people on the phone and trouble shooting anything with a motor. He had an identifying tune that he whistled unconsciously, more or less, all day, "The Tennessee Waltz." When I heard it, I felt a calmness come over me, a feeling that all was right with the world. In all of my years, it's effects never changed or left me. In the early evenings, his little children tumbled around playing on the living room carpet, Uncle Henry drank his big glass of milk, and we all sat glued to the TV while country singers in their sparkly clothes played their guitars and made their forever home in my memory.

I always saw him and my aunt in the summers when I was up visiting my grandparents, the ones with the farm and my grandfather who drank too much. Henry was their only son and had born the brunt of supporting his mother and sister at the tender age of ten during the height of The Depression, delivering papers on his bicycle in the dark mornings of Arkansas cold. And, he continued supporting them long after he was grown and back home from serving as a bombardier in WWII. Hardware was his great love. People felt it. They responded right back, and pretty soon he became one of the most recognized men in town. If there was a problem with anything that needed fixing, folks would say,

— Go on down and see Henry about that.

He managed somehow to make an early life for himself, his sister and his mother in spite of an absent father, and then later on he had the hard job of balancing an unhappy past with an unhappy present when my grandfather showed back up, needing someone to take him in. They had a few rounds of disagreement, the two of them, when his drinking got too bad and it couldn't be ignored anymore. But, we children were kept away from it mostly, although sometimes we did hear raised and angry voices that left unsettling undertones in the air long afterward. The palpable tensions between them never went completely away, but there was a kind of détente that prevailed most of the time. My uncle put a lot of effort into that and worked every one of his days off helping them on the place, fixing and mending, with his wife and children in tow. That's where he spent his time, all of it, helping his folks or working at the hardware store. I never knew him to take a vacation.

But, he was coming to see me now, for two whole days, he and my aunt and their three children, so I had a lot of getting ready to do. Peach had plenty of bedrooms, one for him and Aunt Rose, and two for the kids to share. They just needed a little tidying up, and it was a nice thing to see those rooms all filled again. Ilene and Cynthia made a big thing of it, my family coming to town, and insisted on having one of our big family dinners, just like Peach would have done. It relieved my uncle some, I think, to know that I was alright and safe with these people who were total strangers to us just two years ago. Uncle Henry, more or less, adopted me over the years as one of his own, even though I was way older than his children, and we all had a fine arrangement and even finer memories. He struck gold with Aunt Rose, found a good woman who kept a kitchen warm with fried chicken and mashed potatoes and gravy for lunch, and homemade fudge at Christmas.

He really enjoyed our pecan trees while he was there. We drank our iced tea and sat on our old chairs in the grass and talked and watched as the children ran around the yard, whooped and hollered and played on the rope swing. He and Aunt Rose stayed in one of the big rooms with a tester bed, lace curtains that let in morning sun and blue paper with pale pink peonies. I put a big bouquet of roses and hydrangeas in a pottery pitcher, hand made from good Mississippi clay, over on the dresser. I knew she would like that. She really liked pottery and flowers, especially roses. I think her favorite was The Yellow Rose of Texas that she planted in her own yard at home. And also, she really liked cats, and always had way too many strays around who realized she was an easy touch. We only had barn cats at the farm and they stayed down in the old barn aggressively chasing the rats and mice and occasional snakes, "earning their keep," as Peach used to say. It was a good visit. We talked about Whit, whom he barely knew, and the war and what he thought about the recent events in Chicago and how business was in north Arkansas. And, he made me promise to bring Whit and Isabel up for a visit after he got home, and to bring some of those pecans for Aunt Rose. She made really exceptional pecan pie.

There was a grand ease to it, those small abbreviated days and hours with them. The feeling of being with your people, how lasting the goodness in it was after they had gone. Good-by's were never hard with Uncle Henry. He gave me the comforting sense of everything being alright with the world. I had every confidence that wherever I went on this earth, he would find me, or I would find him, and we would never really be far from each other at all.

Ilene stayed with me the afternoon they drove away, just to keep me and Isabel company, in case I was too sad when they left. And, then she made me come inside and play gin rummy for two hours with the contemplative professor and the lapsed Christian, whom she invited out on a mission of mercy. I was their charity case. Religious people really do rise well to a crisis, and they all tried hard, working at being chatty and encouraging, firmly believing that our fate, Isabels and mine, rested entirely in their hands. I can't remember when we had ever been more cared for. By the end of the evening I on the verge of becoming a contemplative myself, acquiring some sacred relics of my own and planning a pilgrimage to Lourdes. The lapsed Christian became possibly the best version of himself that he had seen in a long time. He was actually doing a good deed. Nothing quite inspired the subtle illusions of sainthood more than helping the less fortunate. There was more to him than he thought, more than any of us thought. There was actually a nice person in there who only needed an opportunity to announce himself. They all did yeoman's work for a couple of hours, lifting me and Doll Baby above the struggles of our earthly trials.

After our enthusiasm for gin rummy began to wane, my care givers slipped away into the night, the fires of sympathy and Christian goodwill sufficiently faded, leaving behind a job well done. Ilene didn't feel that I was adequately unburdened, so she insisted that we both come home with her where we could spend more time in her ministering hands and she could, "get us something decent to eat." She also meant that the evening required something more bracing, the elixir of a warm toddy. That was what she and I both needed, and as usual, Ilene was right. She served them up in two of her monogrammed silver julep cups so they would "stay warm" on an antique tray she found in a vintage shop near the elaborate palazzo, Cá Rezzonico years ago. She adored Venice for many things, its transitory bridges and easy rhythm of life, eating cichetti with locals in a centuries-olds bacaro, strolling the Piazza San Marco and drifting along the Rive degli Schiavoni toward the Doge's palace. But most of all, she loved its opera house, Teatro La Fenice, where she sat transfixed three different times under the baroque spell of *La Traviata*. She made the most of everything, her trips to Venice and Florence, bringing little bits of them home with her for us to enjoy as we were doing now. A diminutive, scrolled Florentine vase holding sprigs of Rosemary and the last blood red roses of summer sat half hidden behind a small, irregular stack of books on my bedside table. I noticed it with my first feeble attempts to open my eyes in the morning, and the faint hint of New Orleans coffee and homemade scones drifting in from the kitchen. Ilene was dedicated to strong coffee, preferably laced with chicory, and waking up to its earthy smell was a divine beginning.

I laid there for a while, too snug, too comfortable to move, soaking in a moment that had no apprehension, no terror in it, but I finally dragged myself free from the warm bed and the tempting embrace of Ilene's pale silk comforter. I struggled into her floppy house shoes and thick terrycloth robe, pulling it around me and contemplating how much effort it would take to make it into the kitchen. Mercifully, it would be a slow morning. Ilene had already done all the heavy lifting and sat Doll Baby in her high chair with a tray full of cereal bits she was shoving between her rosebud lips with her chubby little hands, happy as a clam. Her lavish gift of last night's largess to Isabel and me evidently wasn't all the way over, and Ilene airily flitted around in her floral kimono hovering over me, pouring and buttering and dishing up the substance our souls needed to face whatever this day would bring. She sat down finally across from me in the delicious flood of sunlight that warmed us both all the way through, and we ate our scones with marmalade she made from oranges sent by a friend all the way from his groves down in Indian River. For this one second, everything really was alright with the world, and somewhere, way back in the shadows of my mind, The Tennessee Waltz was playing.

FALL

Our conversations were not idle things, and our letters to each other were the distilled footprints that would later be called history... and perhaps we were all here "for such a time as this."

CHAPTER THIRTEEN

WE THE LIVING

Whit's letters, which came with blessed regularity, filled the information voids, and the voids in our hearts, like water on dry ground. The latest bad news was the death of the night patrol squad on duty securing the camp perimeter. They all died, every single one of them, when a new lieutenant foolishly pursued the enemy beyond the boundaries and out into the dark arms of an ambush from which no one returned. A mortar attack followed and some aircraft were damaged. A few were wounded, but no other casualties. He wrote accounts of each days true events, but I suspected he softened it some. No need to say, "My co-pilot took a round in the chest today that came in right under his chicken plate while we were rocketing a VC village over the Mekong Delta," or, "Six boys died and we lost four helicopters trying to evac A Company up at Tay Ninh." Our local newspaper, The Fontaine Sentinel, was good for a lot of information like that. It usually carried headlines in sensational, attention grabbing, block letters. I looked at the headline for this morning. It read, "Sixteenth Infantry Secures Battle of Loc Ninh." What followed was a mind numbing account of the battle and the body count of VC (Viet Cong) and American forces. Adjoining articles filled the front page, with details of the projected rise in Draft numbers and the stalled Paris Peace Talks. We the living, read all of this from the safety of home. No bloodied soldiers filled our hospital corridors. No rocket fire dimmed the lights. No sirens pierced the night, announcing we were about to be over-run by enemy forces. We slept quiet in our beds, unthreatened by the carnage, and every morning broke open to blue Mississippi skies filled with vagabond clouds drifting high above on impervious currents that seemed to shield us from the worlds disturbances.

We were counting the days now, Whit and I. He would be home in late November, home for the holidays, in time for Thanksgiving and Christmas, both of which he had missed last year. He would actually be with us now, with us at last. Isabel had her own little celebration going. She held a cup all by herself, and she pulled up, holding onto the coffee table and walked all the way around it over and over, gaining both momentum and balance with surprising speed. She had made the amazing discovery of her feet and now seemed as if she was training for an infant marathon she was totally bent on winning. "Never do anything in a small way," was apparently the motto now forming in her little brain. She had, overnight, become mobile. My baby girl had gained her independence, and I had lost mine. Her new mission in life was escape, and I moved on to the next phase of parenthood, preventing her escape. Children were so clever, and their vantage point on the floor was a view with unlimited potential. Electrical plugs, cabinet contents, curtains, trailing plants…no option for exploration was ever off the table. I wrote about all of this to Whit, keeping him up to date on all her little changes. And, Isabel made real baby sounds now. We couldn't wait for her to say mama and daddy.

I made a lot of mistakes, being new at this. I answered the phone one afternoon and foolishly listened to Cynthia for two seconds too long and calamity struck, at least a minor calamity. My gargantuan and newly potted fern that formerly sat on its antique wicker stand on the porch had been strategically repositioned by Doll Baby who only needed two extra seconds to seize the long fronds and pull the whole thing off. She landed in a lap full of dirt, wearing the satisfied expression that came with a task accomplished. She looked up at me, very pleased with herself, enthusiastically caressing the green leaflets and grabbing handfuls of damp black soil, sprinkling it in her hair with a a glorious expression of achievement. She was obviously going to be a plant person. Welcome to your new life, I thought, isn't this going to be fun. Doll Baby's real favorite thing to do now was empty out all of the cabinets in Peach's kitchen. Peach had a lot of interesting things under there, some that probably hadn't been used in decades. There was a metal beater with a handle that spun round and round to make whipped cream I guessed, and a complicated cheese grater, and a big glass container for churning butter. There were giant pots large enough to boil two or three chickens and rolling pins long enough to use as weapons. Doll Baby cleared out all the cabinet contents and stuffed her whole body into the empty space, dragging her pink baby blanket in behind her. That blanket went with her everywhere, and I had to wash it when she was asleep.

We had callers sometimes, distant kin that R. J. turned up roving the countryside, or cousins from some nearby county. These folks were used to stopping by and visiting with Peach. She always gave them a glass of iced tea to drink while they sat and talked on the front porch. One suspicious relative was Edgar Dale, who just appeared every now and then in his old truck with cane poles sticking out of the back. He sometimes brought Peach a string of catfish or crappie from the river. Anna Mae and Willard appeared a few times a year in their large newish car, driving the country roads from Clarksdale, reminding Peach, as others sometimes did, in the warm cadence of afternoon conversation on the porch, that they resided in the heart of "the Delta." Fortunately, I guess, Fontaine at least had the advantage of an earlier founding date than some newer towns. Towns that weren't founded before the "Wo-wa" were perceived as being somewhat lesser in stature and this caused a permanent divide lasting for decades. Even here, there was an unpleasant history with another town over which one became the county seat. The debate was heated and personal. Families were separated, enemies were made, and the conflict cemented itself among the foundational stones of our permanent history. Mostly people just went on with regular life, but occasionally, like down at Donaldson's Hardware and Feed Store, someone said the wrong thing. Somebody else set him straight, and decades of tension came alive, just like the thing, whatever it was, happened yesterday.

These visitors, or pseudo-relatives, felt compelled to carry on their traditions as if Peach was still alive and with us. It couldn't have been because of any obligation to me. This was simply an activity set in stone through years of repetition, and the visitors seemed resistant to any change. They arrived unannounced, got out of their car and knocked on the screen door as they entered.

— Yoo-hoo, we're here, they'd call out.

Then I came out of wherever I was, wondering who "We" were. They sat down in Peach's wicker chairs, fanning themselves and said how it was fifteen degrees hotter than it was at exactly this same time last year, which was my cue to go and fetch the iced tea. Then we talked about the weather first and whether we had too much rain or not enough rain, and the latest family gossip, usually things like Leroy had gotten a new truck, or somebody had a new baby, or some unfortunate soul had "gone to prison for being mixed up in that business over in Georgia." The unfortunate soul, now a felon, was "Uncle Murdock" and we, of course, didn't believe a word of it. He was obviously railroaded, probably by a bunch of damned yankees.

It was so hard to speak ill of our own kin. I marveled at the serpentine labyrinth of verbiage required to extricate our relations from the unpleasant consequences of any wrong doing. The wife, I discovered, after numerous opportunities to participate in these examples of cleansing, was often the most useful culprit, and her obvious shortcomings became the grounds for any future misdeeds.

— She can't even bake a decent pound cake.

— Her people aren't even from around here.

— We all said he was making a big mistake.

— Can you imagine her parading around in shorts on a Sunday?

These phrases were the low hanging fruit, not that these well meaning folks were mean spirited or unchristian. They all really needed only a few basic things; to think well of their people, to be associated with those who were clearly in the right and to enjoy the superior feeling of their position, whatever it was. I offered them all of that. I smiled and nodded and poured their iced tea just like Peach had done and assured them that whatever they just said held the sacred kernels of truth. They never stayed too long, just long enough to unburden their souls and get in a "good visit." I mentioned Whit sometimes and the war in Viet Nam where our boys were fighting and dying. They all shook their heads as if in disbelief that there was any place in the world other than the good north Mississippi ground on which they were currently sitting, the glazed look never leaving their collective faces, and I figured that anything I said probably left their minds before they even reached the bottom step of the porch.

I talked about these visitations with Ilene and Cynthia. They laughed and shared their own experiences with our extended family, most of whom they said were the salt of the earth. There were a couple of cousins from Memphis whom they liked to wine and dine at the country club when they came to town, and they always put them up at their houses and had little soirées with wine and pâté. They knew all about Edgar Dale, the erstwhile relative and fisherman who provided their fish delivery service for years. Ilene even went out in his ragged boat across the river to the old sandbar where there were fish in the deep hole near the rapids. They said he could catch anything with those cane poles of his and he used mostly worms or that vile smelling catfish bait they sold down at the bait house on the river. The personalities dotting the long edges of the Rutledge landscape were pretty clear to me now, and it seemed like almost every day was an education. I tried to amuse Whit with little stories of these encounters, telling him what I said and then what they said, and didn't he think that was funny. I wanted him to feel like he was here sitting on the porch talking with all his folks and not missing out on everyday life here, or what passed for it.

One of the socially well-placed ladies from town asked me what I did all day, and my answers were clearly unsatisfactory. She thought that life out here all by myself was the equivalent of some kind of punishment and coming clear across the river to see me was an act of benevolence like visiting people in jail or widows or the sick. She wore the refined garments of self-sacrifice like a Sunday suit, believing that somehow all this poor girl needed were consistent doses of pity. She had a gift for that. She pitied my location, my circumstances and my lack of appropriate lineage, proper curtains and adequately polished furniture. I wanted to tell her that and it was not as unpleasant out here as it might seem, and she needn't trouble herself with coming all the way to the ends of the earth to see me. But, I just said the usual thing instead.

— Thank you so much, Mrs. Brady. How kind of you to think of me! We'll plan a visit real soon. I'd just love that.

Most of the town ladies felt that this was a sort of no man's land, and their first emotional reaction was sympathy. I was essentially a town person, too, so I understood. Their sporadic visits usually included all kinds of generous advice, assuming that it was their Christian duty to acquaint me with the finer points of home decorating among other things.

— You really need to paint all of this woodwork Dove White. Go talk to Sam down at the paint store. He'll know exactly what you need. Just tell him I sent you. He can get started right away.

— When are you going to put up new drapes on all these windows? You know Lillian's Drapery and Upholstery can make those for you. I'll be glad to have her call you. She can recover these chairs for you, too.

— I'm sure you'll want to replace that sofa. In Bradley's Furniture the other day, I saw one that would be perfect for this room. It was floral with shades of green and blue, and they have an area rug that matches it. I'm sure you'll want everything to look pretty when Whit comes home.

I did like having new things, but Peach's house felt perfect just like it was. It seemed wrong to add things that didn't belong here, like admitting intruders into an atmosphere that was a lifetime in the making. I tended to resist changing the very things that made these surroundings so comforting, so filled with the remnants of her presence here. Nothing in me wanted to change that. I did love the idea of adding new plants to Peach's flower beds though, and it seemed natural, like something she would have done. In the fall I planned to add a new bank of azaleas at the edge of our drive. I became attracted to African violets, especially the doubles with the pale pink frilly blossoms. I bought three small ones at Donaldson's and carefully carried them home in a shallow cardboard box, hoping to not break off any leaves, and put them on the windowsill in the kitchen where they thrived and spilled over in a mad display of enthusiasm.

Late one afternoon I went out to the mailbox to find that the postman came and left three letters for me, one from Whit, one from Charlie and one from a name I didn't know. It was from Bradley's sister in Maine. She said he was wounded and flown to Tokyo for surgery. They'd had no other word about the full extent of his injuries, but his commanding officer wrote them only saying he was shot in a fire fight and had internal injuries. She said Bradley would want me to know, and she would send me his new address as soon as she got it. Whit's letter was worse. That day was spent near the remains of a bombed out, deteriorating villa framed by a wide dike that had once been a road. Surrounded by rice paddies, a platoon gathered on a ridge, the only high ground near the extraction point. Rocket fire dismembered three men in seconds as they dragged their bodies spewing blood into the Huey. The crew were covered, slick with the blood gushing from severed arteries. Back at base it dripped onto the tarmac as the crew chief washed out the helicopter, the color staining the ground in long trails of deep red. It wasn't a good day. Charlie, at least, had good news. They were getting some new pilots. No place to put them yet, but they wouldn't be flying for weeks straight.

The news on TV that night said troop strength was a little over 500,000 with plans to call up over 40,000 more men in the next two weeks. I shuddered a little every time I heard numbers like that. It meant that we were not winning, and a lot more boys would die. Everyone felt that the politicians sold us out, and were looking for a way out. The war that began with such enthusiasm and promises of an easy victory was unpopular now. Men who ran for any office spoke solemnly about our need to get out of Viet Nam before they even introduced themselves. The national sentiment appeared now in the rising smoke of discontent fanned by the flames of anarchy on the streets, and it bled now into the halls of government.

I knew a few other wives whose husbands were "short," counting every single day left in country, and like Whit, down to eight or ten weeks. Balancing the tension between two emotions was way tougher than I imagined. Part of me was thrilled he would be home soon, and part of me was terrified that he wouldn't make it through those last days and hours, maybe dying on the tarmac like those other boys mere minutes from departure. I sat down at Peach's table that evening, like always. I watched a couple of new television variety shows which I liked, and worked on another care package for Whit and Charlie, and sent up some prayers for Bradley, wherever he was, and for his family in Maine. I started on a new needlepoint in colors of pale pink and green for Isabel's room in the house we were going to have some day. This is what we the living do, I thought. This is what we do, just like Miss alma said.

— Honey girl, you've just got to keep on keepin' on, and hope for the best.

161

CHAPTER FOURTEEN

GIFTS OF YESTERDAY

Dreams and shadows were odd things, powerful, yet lacking real substance, unlike actual memories that have a kind of saving power. I recognized the differences between them, and their usefulness, and moved among them all now in a cautionary blend of imagination and reality. I noticed that in the long days of doing everyday things, mundane things, every element of the universe seemed to come to our collective rescue in the thousand ways that couldn't be measured or even told. Hope appeared everyday from the ether of the universe and hovered over us, spreading divine encouragement and supernatural comfort. There was no recognizable joy or faith or even love sometimes, but there was hope. It could be known, and it stayed, long after the other forces I so carefully propagated, slipped elusively away despite my best efforts to hold onto them. The scripture said that, "There are these three: Faith, Hope and Love, but the greatest of these is Love." That must be so, but Hope came to us. It showed up in the darkest hours and I came to rely on it. It came with friends, memories of a past full of shining moments still alive with affection and ease. What comforts the memories of those days were, and reliving them lessened the burden of todays grief. People always said you couldn't live in the past, but I never understood why not, and I never felt it was right to short change the power of a personal history that one day we might need to call on. Why make less of the grand things that, for just one moment, lifted us up above some of our darkest hours of this earth. The past was a gift that could be opened whenever it was needed again, always full of the same comfort and consolation, a perceptible recollection that nothing and no one could take away. I felt that way for as long as I could remember.

Now, on just another uneventful evening in Fontaine, I sat with my feet propped up on Cynthia's sofa in the den while Doll Baby played with her new gigantic pink, stuffed turtle on one of Peach's quilts. It was as big as she was, and she grabbed it with both hands, rolling around with it like an enormous, fluffy playmate. I leaned back against the deep blue cushions, Cynthia's favorite color, and thought about Whit and the first time we met. He came down to the Coast for the weekend with some of his fraternity brothers from Ole Miss, and a mutual friend decided to set him up with "this girl from Gulfport." That turned out to be me, and the morning we got together he planned for us to go up and see the spectacular view of the Gulf from the best vantage point on the Coast, the roof terrace of the Malcolm Hotel. We weren't guests, but he didn't seem daunted by that. I stood there with him there at what felt like the edge of the earth, looking out into the gray fog that came with us. He was comfortably tall, the kind of boy who exuded effortless ease and confidence that managed to spill over everyone around him, and it settled around me like part of the colorless mist obscuring the view we had come here to see. We stood there at the top of the world among the leftover rubble of a party from the evening before that the staff was just beginning to clear, bits and pieces from a festive night scattered at our feet. Hints of the exhilaration still hung in the air, cake crumbs and napkins flung indiscriminately here and there, and I wondered if these remnants of life might be viewed as small pieces of history. Had the partiers paused, looking out into the night beyond the harbor lights into starry darkness above the Gulf and felt the power of the moment, the same primeval connection we were here looking for?

— Come with me. There's something to see that I think you'll appreciate, Whit said first thing that morning, seconds after we met.

We parked on a side street, walked through the vast lobby and came up to the roof for the morning view, that sacred thing that defines the Coast, all blue sometimes above a fading mist. We rode alone in the distilled quiet of an elevator to the top floor, the doors opening finally to a grand vista of hesitant light. The view waited for us out there, as it had for thousands of days and nights, waiting to take our breath away with the grandeur of it, but it eluded us this morning, obscured by the mists we brought with us. Our gray companions were the dripping moss, slate waves and transient fog, low and dense that hung thick in the air, attaching itself to morning on the coast as it often does without warning. I looked out into that semi-opaque world so familiar to me. The mist and I were long acquaintances, and it was here again now, hovering like a luminous blanket shot through with suggestions of sunlight behind it. It lifted when it chose, like a sheer curtain drawn up in a play, slowly revealing a blue symmetry of water and sky. We stood together there, Whit and I, almost friends, waiting for the same thing, waiting for the view to appear before us. But on this morning, the mist came to us as a gift instead, all wrapped in silvery ribbons of attention, simple attention, that obscure and most poorly understood element of all human qualities. How grand to be worthy of someone's attention, I thought. Shy and reticent, it hovered often for an instant, unrecognized, appearing among mortals unaware of its value.

It was really the attention that mattered to me. The invitation was the real gift, sharing the view with someone who appreciated it, who understood the power of its effects on this ground we occupied for our appointed length of days. We weren't disappointed. We came back here on another day, rose to the top floor in the elevator, and walked slowly to the edges of the roof terrace, the slightest separation between us and that view of the beyond, and beyond the beyond. On that day there were no remnants of other parties scattered like tiny jewels at our feet, but we were glad, so glad that for one fated moment in time, we shared the unreserved embrace of celestial light and salt air, and that was our beginning.

Cynthia finally came down the long hall, back to Isabel and me in her ice blue robe fresh from her nightly applications of potions and creams and ready for an old movie. She had a huge bowl of ice cream loaded with nuts and chocolate syrup. I had my own bowl of excessively buttered popcorn and we watched an enthralling actor splendidly tormented by memories of his deceased wife, Rebecca, a British film made from the brilliant and popular novel. It began with a dream of Manderly. From there, life at the country Manor set against the sea near Cornwall had every possibility of capturing our complete attention. No one could surpass his role as Max de Winter. It made me want to be English very badly, to own a Manor House and have servants bring me tea with raspberries and scones every afternoon while I read the Cricket scores in the London Times by a fireplace in the library. How easily the inner yearnings of the heart grow from miniature seeds to embarrassing lushness fed by the merest diet of films and books and music and memories. It was not difficult to picture myself there among the dogs and horses racing about the English countryside, wearing the sensible clothes of the nineteen forties. Some part of me felt that I was living in the wrong decade. I'm not sure Whit knew that about me, that my feet might be squarely planted here in Fontaine, but my soul really lived in another continuum far, far away.

Whitney returned to us late in the evening after Isabel was fast asleep and we were into our double feature of the night and sipping our clandestine wine. His arrival disturbed the pleasant fantasy Cynthia and I had created for ourselves, the one where real life is a gauzy, indistinct thing and the movie and its elevated music transported us to another place entirely. He wanted to talk about football, the game he just came from where the Fontaine Bobcats obliterated some other visiting team, and now they all had visions of a conference championship. He was incredibly enthusiastic, explaining some astonishing pass the quarterback made setting them up for a field goal in the last seconds of the third quarter that put them on the road to a decisive victory. They were heading into the season with two wins and the prospect of another one next week when they traveled to the neighboring town. The coach there was brand new and the previous season's outstanding quarterback graduated and was now an emerging powerhouse at State. Cynthia and I understood completely. The whole town was plastered now with blue and white posters of the Bobcat Football Schedule, and the boys on the football team enjoyed the benefits of being local celebrities. If one of them even drove by in his car, someone called out to get his attention.

— Oh look, there goes Billy Ray. You know he's a wide receiver.

And, they would wave real big like they were lifelong friends and shout in his direction.

— We're all cheering for you, Billy Ray!

These boys perfected the swagger they had worked on since they were old enough to hold a baseball bat, strolling around town in the sunshine of adoration, a girl on each arm, and each one after his Football jacket. A girl who was going steady with a football player had real status, and she made sure everybody knew it. Her folks did, too. She wore his letter jacket that totally engulfed her and hung clear down past her hips rain or shine. When the relationship deteriorated, usually because of some seductive and conniving rival, he asked her to give back his jacket, and she was a wreck for weeks. Going out without that jacket now was practically like being naked. Everybody knew they had broken up, and the tragedy had to be handled in just the right way or hard feelings might spill out among the parents. In some cases there would never be any forgiveness. The aftermath of this heartbreak had remarkable survival skills. It might reappear in fifteen years when the now married matron found herself overtaken one morning by the sudden, raw emotion of it, the shy, surviving sentiment that brought sudden and unexpected tears to her eyes while she was frying bacon and making school lunches in a gray dawn. She would always remember him, remember his face and that letter jacket she wore. She was that girl again for just an instant, that smiling, popular girl people envied and admired. This was the stuff of dreams, not forgotten, not discounted, but kept close forever, remembered days hidden in the deep recesses of a life beyond the reach of human ruin, safe from the vandalism of unfriendly words.

I ran into this kind of thing myself a few times, even now. Someone's mother couldn't resist telling me how hurt their little girl had been when Whit broke up with her. I struggled to know what to say to that so I finally settled on a phrase that would illicit consolation.

—I know just what you mean. When my first boyfriend broke up with me, it just broke my heart. It took me a long time to get over it.

That seemed to provoke enough sympathy to smooth things over. I had suffered, too, and for some reason that made her feel better. My own obvious need for condolence made it easier for her to view me with a lesser degree of animosity and a greater degree of pity. There was, it seemed to me, a dark, primal inclination in the human nature of some people, an irresistible desire to just take someone down a peg, to make them feel guilty of some imagined fault or less than they might actually be, and I was apparently a tempting and easy target. Simply limiting the satisfaction level of my interrogator was my own small act of resistance, and the semi-isolation of Peach's house did have advantages, because I had less exposure to conversations just like that.

R. J. and the boys were up to their necks harvesting cotton. I rarely saw Cash. Everybody worked day and night, and the trucks kept up a steady cloud of dust on the road going in and out. His fields of Upland cotton were irrigated, so they avoided some of the problems that came with insufficient rain, and he thought they might come close to a thousand pounds per acre this year. He was so busy that sometimes he even missed church which meant that Isabel and I had the opportunity to slip down to Father Ed's with Ilene and try out her church. For some reason which I didn't fully understand, it seemed to fit me better. R. J. always encouraged my religious outings with Ilene. I think he felt that I was always safe with her, and whatever we did was alright with him. Between football and cotton he had his hands full, but we talked almost everyday. He kept a close watch on the farm, and sold off some of the cows. He was thinking of planting soybeans and thought the house might need a new roof soon. He had a crew to harvest the pecans in a couple of months and the hay barn was almost full, just everyday life in the country. Probably, he never had two seconds to reflect on or re-live the past like I did, when I noticed that the Gulf was too far away to hear it like I needed to today. The idea would have seemed foreign, maybe even a colossal waste of time. He was a man who lived in a seamless present and was perfectly suited for it in every way. Probably he had a lot of A. W., his dad, in him, and this feel for the land captured him the very beginning.

Meanwhile in Paris, in a world separated from Fontaine by half of a continent and an entire ocean, delegations and diplomats of the Vietnam peace talks were still disgruntled over whether the negotiating tables should be square, round, rectangular or diamond shaped. Hanoi apparently insisted on a square table and South Vietnam proposed another shape entirely. To date there were nine configurations being debated by the different delegations. A unilateral halt in bombing was being hinted at by American sources. This fig leaf was hopefully designed to encourage the parties back toward serious negotiation, but it seemed more and more that the world had been sold an overly optimistic view of bringing the two sides to any serious resolution. Major newspapers desperately sought clever ways around actually saying that the peace talks were at a stalemate. Our own headline at the Sentinel said, "Slight Gains At Peace Talks." Compounding the difficulties in Paris, the student protests spilled out to the Sorbonne and the Latin Quarter. Thousands of demonstrators barricaded the streets, assaulting police with

169

cobble stones night after night in the hot spotlight of coverage by an international press. The war casualties at home continued to mount. According to the paper, the count hovered now around fourteen thousand for the year so far, the ranks of servicemen now being supplemented by roughly three thousand boys a month whose draft numbers came up. And, here in Fontaine, we all held our collective breath, hoping to be spared another afternoon burying one of our boys in the dark soil of Fernwood.

I had taken to reading self-improvement articles, the kind found in various women's magazines that explain how to become a more confident and sophisticated version of yourself. Apparently, the whole world was in need of such guidance because these pieces appeared in some form in almost every magazine issue and even in popular books; "Change Your Life Now," "Five Steps to Inner Strength," "The Hidden Path to Self-Awareness." All of these were just the tip of the iceberg. Was there really a vast multitude out there who felt their insecurities as deeply as I did? It didn't seem so to me. All of the people I knew seemed quite settled, quite ordinary and unencumbered by the dark clouds of self reflection. I knew my problems well enough. For one thing, I was too young and inexperienced, too raw. I felt the pinpricks of criticism too deeply, so it was easier to avoid the discomfort of company. Whit puzzled me because he did not seem at all put off by my insecurities, in fact, he appeared not to see them at all. But he was gone from me now, and there were demons I had to fight on my own. The dark seeds of self doubt were planted early in me I suspected, for I had known them all my life, and now they had flowered and born fruit, and I was harvesting them with the same methodic intensity that R. J. was harvesting cotton.

I especially disliked artificial snobbery, where lines were indelibly drawn between who was "in" and who was "out," the kind where some person pretends to be your new best friend and then betrays your little confidences at the very first opportunity, when the sharing of information previously unknown is simply too great a temptation to resist.

— I know I shouldn't be telling you this...and promise me that you won't tell a soul, but the other day I heard that....

In the current parlance, that was called gossip and it appeared to be the daily food of quite a few, having been raised to practically an art form by the obsequious Etta Banks. It disturbed me a little, being seated next to her at that charity dinner down at the Elks Club. Her narrow pig eyes, startling blue and thick with mascara, flashed like howitzers, alert to any potential target, always looking for someone to dissect, prying out information that she could use later like ammunition. She hunted with the unquenchable appetite of an urban carnivore and ate people alive while they were still breathing, barely pausing before moving on to her next meal, delicately consuming each dainty portion of flesh. No moment was sacred, no conversation valued as anything more than an energetic fishing expedition. My father, a lovely man, hated this kind of thing, and now I hated it, too, which was a problem because life in a small Southern town was insufficiently interesting without daily bits of gossip to feed on.

I was startled to learn a while later that Etta Banks had succeeded in attracting the attentions of some pale and harmless young man from Atlanta who apparently thought her domineering ways were an endearing feminine aberration. Her family invited him to visit Fontaine where Etta Banks clung to his arm and dragged him all over town to show him off to everyone. Fortunately, he came from a long family line of accountants, short and reserved, sporting an anemic mustache in vain search of victory on his thin upper lip. Severely attired in a gray suit designed to emphasize steadiness and discretion, he possessed all of their ancestral restraint with no proclivity for daring or imagination, the epitome of mildness and tolerance. He was perfect. I pictured him in his office at a suitably expansive desk, blinking behind his glasses, nodding gravely at risk patterns and actuarial tables and signing checks for Etta's ridiculous extravagance. Two full columns in the newspaper announced their engagement and plans for a gaudy June wedding. By this time next year Etta Banks would be firmly installed among the city's young matrons, and she would be their problem. I did admire her ability to always land on her feet, though. Possibly, within the fertile boundaries of her new territory, she would find two or three others exactly like herself, and in a few short years they would be efficiently running the city of Atlanta.

Even the Rebel Dip was a hot bed of colorful local gossip, and could be entertaining in a way. But, I didn't really enjoy hearing all of it too much because I wondered what they said about me after I had gone. Did someone speculate about the diluted energies that might characterize life at the end of a country road?

— Well, she just stays out there on that farm too much. It's not healthy, poor girl. No wonder she's so quiet. The Librarian, Darnelle, says that she checks out six books at a time every few days, so she must read a lot. But, she reads people I never heard of, stuff by a lot of foreigners.

Maybe they voiced suspicions that were much worse. I didn't know what people thought about me, but I was pretty sure I had a friend in Mr. Wade. We understood one another, bound by the same deep fears, nurturing the same smoldering embers of hope that required constant fanning to keep the small struggling flame alive. How much it took everyday to do that, to keep hope alive. When he came out of the kitchen we sat together in one of his red plastic booths that stuck to bare legs, with errant French fries underneath the formica table that had escaped Ray Don's probing broom. We always had versions of the same conversation, dusting off the words to make them seem less artificial.

— How is Lyle? Are they still deployed near Khe Sahn? Any word about pulling them out?

— Yes, he said they had a new first Lieutenant, and they were moving back toward their resupply base in the next few days where they would get more mail and new C rations.

He described Lyle's C rations...he said each one had one canned meat, one canned fruit, bread or dessert and an accessory packet with cigarettes, matches, chewing gum, toilet paper, coffee, cream, sugar, salt, and a spoon. The troops out deep in the jungles lived daily on C rations. Lyle said the meat choices were usually Beefsteak, Beans and Wieners, Meatloaf and Boned Chicken, but the new rations would have Ham Slices and Turkey Loaf. He was hungry for something close to good country ham, and there were tins of new desserts; pound cake and pecan roll. Lyle missed his daddy's cooking and didn't spend a day without remembering the smells of chicken frying in the deep baskets or yeast rolls hot out of the oven in the kitchen at the Rebel Dip. Darlene, I noticed, had a new shorter haircut that tucked behind her ears, and she hustled around with the weary look of someone who was just about on her last nerve. Juggling her concern about Ray Don, the new expense of her daughter's drill team uniform and the intermittent absence of her sometimes alcoholic husband was a full time job all by itself. He had exhausted her sympathetic nature some time ago, and now often found consolation with a bottle in the forgiving dimness of some bar or motel. The world, it seemed had an endless supply of lonely women with hard luck stories, clinging to the edge of disaster, and he managed, regularly, to be the savior they were looking for. Darlene gave up trying years ago and now she was just mad and tired of living in a trailer on the edge of her grandfathers forty acres. She still clung to dreams of a little house in town and a kitchen with running water that came out of the faucet all the time, and not just sometimes. The pump to the well wasn't exactly dependable, failed often in the winter, and she finally figured out how to get it started again, usually in the inopportune cold of a dark night surrounded by the glowing eyes of coons in the corn field. It was a perpetual reminder that the husband who dazzled her with his newish pickup and raw good looks wasn't dependable either, and nothing on God's green earth was going to change that. Every one of us had our own burdens and we were, all of us, unified in one thing, just trying real hard to keep a brave face on it. We all did our part, and mostly we succeeded.

CHAPTER FIFTEEN

A UNIVERSE AFIRE

"How I miss everyone and look forward to the holidays when I will be home with you all at last. We were shelled last night and the enemy keeps probing our defenses night after night, but so far they haven't been able to penetrate our perimeter. We had a real fight on our hands today and took fire along the Mekong river again. My crew chief counted forty-seven holes in our aircraft when we got back in. Some of the others were worse. Maintenance is working day and night to keep us all in the air, or at least most of us. A chinook finally brought in the ship that was shot down in that rice paddy that I told you about. Can't believe they walked away from that one. They completely lost the tail boom. Sorry to hear about Bradley. I hope he will be okay. The medical care here on the front lines is not bad and they get the wounded out pretty quick. Give my love to everyone, especially Doll Baby. Don't let her forget her daddy. I'll be home soon now to both of you. How I miss my girls. Forty-six more days. We are short ! Love, Whit."

That was part of yesterday's letter, and I began to sense his excitement at being now so close to the end. He started to see himself in the autumn here, trodding the sloping paths on fire with red, the sleeping fields of amber vegetation at rest, and the opal

mists ascending like wood smoke at dusk. There was a peace in it, in the canopy of oaks and pecans, elms and chestnuts and wild trees that adopted our forest, springing from some invisible origins and promises of hallowed life. The tawny woods rose all around, full of color, alive with the power of primal instincts that prevailed against all the odds of nature, bound together in marriages of convenience by aggressive vines reaching in some places to the sky. The shy creeping tendrils of wood vine crowding the winding paths no longer bore the eccentric blossoms of summer. Those were gone now, and the branchlets marched on alone as if in revolution, refusing to acknowledge the departure of their formerly attached companions. They ascended the miniature landscape as irregular fraternities advancing their voiceless message: Let us go on alone, even if we do not flower.

The insolent web of trumpet vines, known to us for their startling orange blooms and voracious appetites, thrust their barbaric fingers upward toward the sky, making prisoners of leaning pines, birch and ironwood. Mayhaws hid down in the river bottoms thick with tupelo gum and hawthorn. Once, long ago, making jelly from the red fruit occupied the warm days of April and May until the thorny thickets became an impassable barrier to mortal advancement. The scant paths worn narrow now by the daily roaming of rabbits and deer, possums and foxes wound here and there among the brittle grass or beneath the tangled overgrowth of hollies and thistles and fallen branches. Whit and I walked here before, bending low beneath the hanging limbs that threatened to obscure the path, and surveyed the patterns of light that crept across the carpet of leaves falling like paper rain from high above. Our innocent roamings left the dank smell of earthen moss around us, the scent clinging to our boots and clothes, the residue of a primal quietude of decaying blossoms, helianthus and Indian tobacco.

The first cold breath of fall came upon us all. Those crimson and gold days I longed for, prayed for, arrived in an aggressive morning chill that prompted the trees to begin dropping their leaves almost in unison. It was unseasonal. Everyone said so. Usually fall crept in with the genteel aloofness of ornamental stealth and gave us all plenty of time to adjust to it, football weather, a subtle beginning signaling that the season would not be presumptuous or demanding. The brazen summer left us a little worn and tired, yearning for the ease of harvest moons and mown hay. The mere opening of Peach's mammoth walnut chest, full of quilts and family history and wool sweaters evoked the scent and promise equal to the fabled genie in a bottle, the genie of fall. I stood before it, breathing in the first raw hint of the cedar lining, and looked down at the dark stacks folded in those even rows, the narrow leather boxes of faded photographs tied with narrow satin ribbons, the quilts all made with Peach's own hands. She stood right here in this exact spot a year ago, folding and tidying and arranging everything in this chest until it was just right, ready and waiting for the next season, and now it was upon us. Only, she was not here to reach for the long gray sweater that held deep pockets of pecans gathered on a morning walk at first light, or gather up the quilt in the wedding ring pattern in blues and greens, just the right weight for the bed now. A year ago, she had pulled it from the stack, shaken it and taken it out to air on the porch to freshen it, laid across the long wicker chaise. I half expected the contents of the chest to stir in resistance at the strange face peering down at them. Her smiling face saw them all. Her worn hands lovingly touched them all for fifty years, and now my face appeared here, reaching into a world that was hers. I picked up Doll Baby and pointed down at the chest.

— Look. See those quilts? See those sweaters? Those belong to Peach. Can you say, Peach?

If Peach was somewhere looking down, I hoped that she smiled seeing us there together, the inheritors of all that she had left us. I wondered if fifty years from now, some strange girl would lift my things from this chest and remember my life here. In a hundred years, there would be no one who recalled these days of our mortality, who remembered us at all, no recollections of this year we all endured, our struggles, our intransigent griefs and our little hard won triumphs. Doll Baby and I finally pulled the wedding ring quilt from its place in the stack and carried it out to the porch, spreading the heavy folds out over the long chaise as Peach did. That evening, when the last of this days light slipped away, I smoothed it out over my bed and felt the weight of it settle over me, covering me as it had covered her for years and years.

I finally had the courage to paint her kitchen a pale green the color of faded moss instead of the yellow I had planned. It actually looked pretty surrounded by all of the green wall papered rooms. It felt fresh and brought the green extravagance of her flowerbeds inside and reflected the warm light that poured in through the long windows and white tie-backs around the breakfast table.

Cash helped me. He brought samples out from town for us to try and then stood back with me to analyze our choices. He liked being in her kitchen, doing something for her that she would have liked. We both did. In the end, as the new green rose slowly up the walls, there was a rightness to it, and we suspected that we had done it for her even more than we had done it for ourselves. He was so proud of our accomplishment. It was a first for both of us. It was more than a beginning for him, for his rustic visions of horses and pastures and stalls of blooded stock, everything this place could be.

Now that I was the acting custodian of her recipe box, I became addicted to its contents. Every recipe card and scrap of paper now yellowed and brown with age was written in her even, slanted hand. It was informally organized, and for many things she didn't even need a recipe. But, I felt she surely knew where every recipe could be found in that box. I spread them all out on the dinning room table to better examine the contents; Chess Pie, Lemon Meringue Pie, Blackberry Jam Cake, Pound Cake, Banana Bread, Squash Casserole, Corn Fritters, Homemade Bread and Butter Pickles, Creole Egg Casserole, Pimento Cheese, Peach Ice Cream, Preachers Pralines, Chicken Stew, Chicken Pot Pie, Gumbo, Tomato Aspic, Dew Berry Jam. There were many more, and she had several cookbooks, too, from various Ladies Auxiliaries and churches around Mississippi. They were worn and falling apart, the pages ragged from decades of use, all evidence of years of Rutledge meals, a culinary history of life here in this place. These were the finest offerings of legions of club women and church ladies who left their best recipes behind them to grace other Southern tables, a legacy we were all lucky enough to inherit.

One cookbook was titled, "A Year of Casseroles." Nearly every recipe seemed to have either cream of mushroom or cream of chicken soup as a foundational ingredient. There was chicken with cream of chicken soup and asparagus topped with grated cheese and crumbled ritz crackers. Hot Chicken Salad had mayonnaise, celery, pecans and grated cheese topped with crushed potato chips. Curried chicken was chicken breast layered over broccoli smothered in cream of mushroom soup and sour cream. There was a casserole for every single day. The cookbook author helpfully answered the big question facing us all at one time or another: What to fix for dinner. Another cookbook from a church over in the Delta began with a description of geography, reminding its readers that the Delta begins in a famed hotel lobby in Memphis and ends on Catfish Row in Vicksburg. These recipes descended from the first settlers arriving in 1825, the landed pioneers carving a future in this primordial land of forests and cane breaks. Its pages were filled with recipes for Venison Roast, Wild Duck, Oyster Stuffed Turkey, Turtle Bisque, Watermelon Pickles, Cheese Straws, Cabinet Pudding and thirty-two different kinds of cakes. It was like reading history, and made me want to immediately cook one of everything in it. Menu's were arranged with appropriate recipes for every occasion and every holiday with helpful tips on what time each meal should be served. "Brunch on the Veranda" began at 11:00 a.m. with Creole Stuffed Eggs, Pineapple Fritters and Vicksburg Baked Ham and Biscuits, and ended with Diablo Coffee and Lemon Custard Cake with Raspberry Sauce laced with Peach Brandy. It suggested itself as the holy grail of recipes, and I wanted a taste of everything, imagining myself wearing a flowing romantic frock reclined in a wicker chair on a veranda nibbling one of those pineapple fritters.

I was so fond of reading Peach's cookbooks and recipes that I decided to begin collecting my own. Once a week the Sentinel included a food column featuring four or five recipes, so I decided to paste them into the heavy black pages of a scrapbook. It was my own hesitant beginning. There were always recipes in women's magazine's, so I began collecting those, too. Cutting those out and arranging them in my own work in progress cookbook was satisfying. It was a window to another delicious world full of new things to try. My first pages had recipes for Divinity, Chicken N' Dumplings, Fresh Apple Cake, Jambalaya, Homemade Bread, Meatloaf, and Stuffed Cornish Game Hens. My cutting and pasting became a nightly thing and I hoped, by the time Whit came home, my personal cookbook would be as substantial and as delicious as Peach's own collection of recipes.

A letter came a few days ago from Maine. Bradley's sister wrote to say that he was coming home and would be in a hospital in D.C. His parents planned to fly up from Tuscaloosa to be there when he arrived. They were all broken up she said, worried, and in ill health themselves, but trying their best to manage. Her children were in school, but she arranged for them to stay with friends so she could get away herself. That was all the information there was right now, and she said she would let me know more later. At least he is coming home, I thought. At least he's alive. There would be time enough to sort out his recovery later and maybe before long he would be back in Alabama, living near his parents on Cherry Street. It seemed that all the talk in Washington about halting the bombing of the North only emboldened the enemy and made the war more dangerous. They could re-supply now, strengthening their positions without fear of bombing. Possibly Bradley had been a victim of this newly created approach that seemed primarily crafted to give politicians cover in an election year.

The flames of war burned as bright as ever. The latest bold headline in the Sentinel announced, "Enemy Assaults Fire Base Rhonda." The war ended up right in their laps that night. Over eight hundred North Vietnamese poured over the razor wire perimeter into our howitzers firing point blank through the darkness until air strikes began in the first early light. It was a blood bath, the choppers finally able to take out the dead and wounded in daylight and bring in fresh replacements. The paper said twelve men were killed and over fifty wounded. Fire Base Rhonda was only one of many small, isolated forward positions miles away from a battalion's base camp, the scene of battles that raged on night after night. Other headlines in The Sentinel burned just as bright, "Protests Turn Violent in Birmingham." The civil rights marches in cities throughout the South brought the smoke filled streets and clashes with the police right across our television screens. It was carnage, too, just of a different sort. The paper carried an editorial about Marks, a small town not far from Fontaine and the Mule Train and Poor Peoples Campaign that earlier had made it all the way to an encampment called Resurrection City on the National Mall in Washington, D. C. The poverty in Marks, Mississippi drove many to tears. There was still turmoil swirling around the riots that happened down at Ole Miss five years ago. It kept the journalists busy. There was plenty of news to cover, too much. As every day closed around us, we never knew what storm of bad news waited for us on the horizon.

R. J. just about had all his cotton in, and everyone breathed a sigh of relief now. Bobcat football continued its meteoric rise, to the joy and consternation of friend and foe. It was usual to hear conversations that began, " I knew we were going to have a team this year." And, the games at State and Ole Miss were hotly discussed. Whitney felt that the Ole Miss defensive line was weak, and R. J. grumbled about State's coaching staff, nodding in agreement with other men whose appetite for football never waned. They dissected Georgia's sports program and held their own strong opinions about Alabama and Auburn. Our Homecoming Parade was suitably extravagant. The little Queen and her court rode down our main street in splendid convertibles furnished by the Civitan Club. The queen this year was a cousin of the Garden Club queen. That was quite a bit of royalty for just one family, and it kept the mothers busy outfitting the girls for the accompanying social events. The Homecoming Queen wore a pale pink suit with a corsage of yellow roses at her Royal Court Luncheon, while the Garden Club Queen wore a pale yellow suit and a corsage of pale pink roses at her Queens Luncheon. Both events were held in the Country Club dining room decorated with pine and cedar garlands and mums the size of dinner plates. I thought about Isabel and wondered if possibly she might one day be Queen material. She would have the good looks for it. I could already see that, and the requisite bubbly personality. Cynthia would have quite a time decking her out with trips to Memphis or maybe even New York. She might already be planning it right now. It wouldn't surprise me. It gave her something to look forward to, something to do.

At the farm, my mornings were mostly for working, but evenings alone had a lot of hours in them, too many. So, I sat in Peach's rocker and sifted through my tidal basin of thoughts, assessing each shell and fragment for its qualities. In my own estimation, the refracted light illuminating the miniature activities of our daily lives here bore little resemblance to the dark and ominous shadows dominating the landscapes of other town and cities, the existences of other places worlds away. In Paris, London, Santiago, Calcutta, Budapest, Algiers and Berlin rallies and riots broke out honoring the passing of one of their revolutionary heroes. He was just brutally executed in Bolivia and now guerrilla groups everywhere donned his trademark dress, faded military fatigues, black berets and beards. A Cuban leaders impassioned eulogy implored the people to live on embodied by the spirit of their deceased comrade in three full days of mourning. On October 18, a million Cubans gathered in Havana's Plaza de la Revolución to honor their fallen revolutionary. I thought he was not completely wrong at the beginning. He was a young medical student torn by the hunger, poverty and disease that flourished throughout South America, and hoped the Cuban Revolution, overthrowing Batista, was the beginning of change. Now, college students across the nation and across the world, emboldened by his untimely death, found themselves a cause worthy of protest. They all seized the moment, riding the prevailing winds of transformation, their strident and fiery pronouncements rising on the contested streets and campuses, ripe for change.

Such passions found no home here, no fertile place to take root in the rural farms and fields of Mississippi. Within Fontaine and its proximities there were simply no willing antagonists to be found anywhere. Whatever the struggles were in South America, life here in America was not given to revolution at this moment, but to another form of survival, a grand simplicity of souls united now in one great wish for our boys to return to us. I thought about the spirit who rises from the dead in the story of "Our Town, " rich with the imaginations of the author. The young woman in the story, newly passed away, returned as a spirit to visit her old life, watching her mother make breakfast in the kitchen, listening to her father talk about her birthday present, and was distraught by the fact that they couldn't see her. Her plea was for the living, that within the mundane movements of each life we actually 'saw' each other, that we made the most of simple moments when we sat together in the warmth of a kitchen and read a newspaper and drank coffee. If that could be true, if I came back here in the afterlife and watched my current self looking through Peach's recipes at her dining room table, or setting out her Blue Willow china or airing out her quilts and winter sweaters, would I be happy? Would I smile at myself sleeping under her quilts or walking out under the spreading bows of her groves or putting pecans into the deep pockets of her gray sweater that was a little long for me? Would I be glad, so glad for a task that had some nobility in it? I thought so. I believed the hours and days we lived required something more. They deserved to be noticed. Our conversations were not idle things, and our letters to each other were the distilled footprints that would later be called history. Fontaine was our town, and perhaps we all were here, "for such a time as this."

CHAPTER SIXTEEN

DOES HEAVEN REACH THIS FAR

I didn't know him or his people, the boy who died. They were from the part of the county that bordered Water Valley over to the east, in the green recess of forests that cling to the edges of meandering waters named long ago by the Choctaws. He grew up here, roamed and hunted these hills, and now he would be laid to rest at Fernwood. According to the obituary column in the paper, Corporal Gilbert Winston died of injuries at the 8th Field Hospital at Nha Trang. He was survived by parents, two brothers, a sister, grandparents and assorted cousins. They now bore a grief that would never go away. He would be remembered and mourned as long as they all drew a breath. I knew that Whit had flown wounded soldiers up to Nha Trang on the coast. Perhaps Corporal Winston had been injured in the same battle where Whit might have been, in Da Lat or Xuan Loc or Vung Tau, names he mentioned often. Whit might have carried him out of a watery grave with a load of others, headed away from the blood and the stench of battle. Reading the names of the deceased seemed so artificial, as if this person existed entirely now as a statistic duly recorded in black and white newsprint. He had a life for twenty-two years. I thought, how could he have known that twenty-two years were all that he would have.

It was another sad day in Fontaine. The funeral procession fell in behind the long black hearse winding up Washington Street, past

Donaldson's Hardware and Feed Store, past Well's Department Store and the Ideal Shop and Spenser's Drugs. As they passed, the sidewalks grew silent. Men removed their hats, and the faint touch of tangible grief we all tried desperately to avoid hung in the light morning breeze over the procession of mourners. They moved slowly on up the hill past the resting rose gardens and willows that clung to the edges of the river park toward Fernwood. There, Gilbert was laid to rest among the crisp, fallen leaves and new chrysanthemums decorating the earth for his arrival. He was at peace now, free from the horrors of war. He had watched the fury of mortars at Dong Tâm shelling elements of the 9th Infantry in a starless night not fifty yards away from his Navy River Patrol Boat gliding slowly in the dark recesses of the Mekong. And, then the boat hit an enemy mine, erupting instantly in a cascade of fire that exploded upward toward a retreating moon taking him and the entire crew with it. The mangled pieces of bodies drifted, draining blood in the slow currents along the riverbanks until the helicopters came. The Dustoff crews pulled the wounded and the dead from the dark waters and turned for the Field Hospital at Nha Trang. Gilbert was a radio operator, they said, on a PBR in the IV Corps area south of Saigon. He died the next day, his badly burned body finally giving up and his soul slipping away with countless others, rising from the blood soaked ground together.

There was always talk at Estelle's when one of our boys died. Commiserations were the proper term for it. It was not necessary to have known a soldier or his people to feel a deep and haunting sense of loss. Something fine had been taken away and was gone now from the increasingly fragile fabric of our town, and we were all the worse for it. I quietly felt for a long time that there were spirits all around us in some world that we could not see. Their visitations suggested unspoken sympathies that drifted in on gentle currents if a person was paying attention. I could say that I "saw" them on occasion, beckoning to me in a pale morning mist or the awakening at first light. They seemed always solicitous and trying, in their way, to guide me into some realm of awareness previously unknown to me. They formed gentle gatherings sometimes, irregular groups, their arms outstretched as if to welcome a newly departed being, anxious to comfort and soothe the newly released soul. I sensed their presence often when I looked out at the blue edges of the Coast, perhaps they were here to welcome the lost, or comfort the disquieted. A faint warmth and benevolence characterized the spirits from this other world, and it was not difficult at all to embrace the generosity sent to me from beyond. How grateful I was for it. I thought of them as I stood with the other mourners now beneath the ancient trees at Fernwood and had that light impression of the spirit assemblage around Gilbert's newly dug grave, perhaps his distant kin, or even angels, waiting to gather him to themselves. How many other souls, I wondered, yearned for things we cannot see.

His people, stricken with grief, stood weeping around his casket. He rested there now in the white satin lining of the dark wood box, wearing his uniform on the last journey, the one that took him, not into war or to a movie with his girlfriend or to Sunday dinner with his family, but into Eternity. Those opportunities were lost to him and all the others now. I walked away finally, away from the raw grief of it, threading my way down the sloping path among the headstones announcing that people had lived and died here, and other monuments told the stories of the ones who mourned them and lived on for years and years until they, too, were laid to rest here. Some of the inscriptions were Bible verses like, "The Lord is my Shepherd; I shall not Want." Other stones of faded words reflected the depths of human love : "She was our Light and will not be Forgotten," "Sweet Child, Our Joy, Taken Too Soon, Rest Now In The Arms Of The Lord," " Rest Is thine; Sweet Remembrance Ours." The memorials of these departed souls constituted a city within a city, its population joined now by the common thread of eternal bonds.

Fernwood existed as a hallowed ground of aged wrought iron, ancient oaks, azaleas, roses and narrow paths where somehow the compelling significance of each life was sustained. Corporal Winstons parents, Gaston and Lavinia, his brothers Charles and Roland and his younger sister Bonnie all became different versions of themselves when he left them. I went to Cynthia's to pick up Doll Baby and then home to an empty house where, for all of us, hope was still alive. But, they all went home to that empty place where Gilbert used to be. Food was waiting for them there on the long kitchen tables; fried chicken and deviled eggs and buttermilk pie, the usual funeral fare, over-filling the counters crowded with sliced ham, casseroles and more pies and cakes, enough food to feed a small army, or sustain a family in mourning. Their people all came to share their grief, the solemn offerings of comfort and sympathy. I remembered how it was when Peach left us, the futility of it. No amount of consolation, no amount of effort could take the place of someone whose personal presence was now absent. Gilbert and Peach lived on now in a new place among the departed, in memories kept alive by affections that do not die, and in an instant, we who remained became both beneficiaries and custodians of all that they left behind them.

Out at the farm the pecans were falling now, released by nature to come back to this earth, reminders that there is a God in Heaven. The seasons continued, unhindered by death or disillusionment. Flowers gloriously bloomed and faded. The fields of new mown hay lived on, fragrant and newly resurrected now in a cavernous barn with Cistercian sanctity, a humble cathedral of acolyte cats and transmigratory mice. I came and sat here, breathed in the scent of it sometimes and wondered if I should light a candle, offering up the incense of prayers for the living, remembering the souls who were lost to us and pledging remembrance. Did we the living deserve such holy orders? Does Heaven reach this far? When I thought of Whit, prayed for him, the words came up from the depths as if awaiting their turn, waiting for their moment to be spoken. Grand prayers seem to rise in the gallant hours, celebrated in old traditions on ancient steps or hallowed ground by eloquent men prepared for these eternal appointments. But, what pleadings came from us, the simply consecrated, known only to the celestial sphere by the deep cry of our hearts, heavy with the vernacular of the desperate that rose upward from forlorn footpaths or silent cemeteries or scented hay toward the heavens? I believed with the confidence of the young, that Peach's prayers, and mine, had been spoken and were gone out from us now into the beyond and lingered there, awaiting their moment to be heard.

The farm was becoming a different place now, lying fallow in the stealthy shadows that descended upon us at the chill edges of winter, the gray suggestions of primal sleep that nature recognizes in the ragged curves of forgotten green, now shriveled against the moss. The snowballs, retiring now, hung spent and gray beside the oak leaf hydrangeas dripping their forgotten blooms. The friendly roses, violets and unrefined honeysuckle became forlorn things of the past, leaving behind the lonely decaying foliage to tell the story of the year that had been. I cut back the wandering vines and wilted stems that had begun with such enthusiasm in the spring. They were eager now to sleep undisturbed in the dark earth beneath blankets of fresh pine straw I raked into large irregular piles. The persistent pecan limbs and oak leaves, dropping from high above, sprinkled an untidy rebellion upon our small oasis, an omnipresent reminder of natures wild intentions. Isabel and I gathered pecans, too. She was mobile now in an unsteady way, but gaining confidence with every step. I pulled her along the path down to the barn in her little red wagon, a miniature adventure, and she loved the cows, reaching through the fence to touch their warm, furry sides. I bequeathed our flock of chickens to Miss Alma to mingle with hers and we made periodic pilgrimages to visit them all. They flourished under her care and became prolific egg producers. Isabel thought that throwing tiny handfuls of chicken feed into the pen was very entertaining. Before long, Miss Alma would be leading her by the hand out to the chicken coops and teaching her how to gather the warm eggs from the straw filled nesting boxes.

There was news from town. Mr. Wade had a letter from Lyle. It looked like he would be home before Christmas, maybe leaving from Cam Ranh Bay. Whit's letters all had short numbers on them now, 20 days, 19 days, 18 days. It seemed like a miracle, being so close to the end, and we all began to think and feel differently. Cynthia visibly changed, the burden of fear she had born all these months began to lift. She smiled more and talked about Whit as if he had merely gone into town on an errand and would be back, walking through the door any minute. Whitney looked a lot less grim and began to relax, losing himself in the entertaining statistics of college football and who was playing in the Bowl games. We watched the nightly news on TV each evening, the battles, the body count of dead and wounded , the latest protests and clashes with police, but now the weight of it began to lift.

Whit was coming home, and the battles in those places far away couldn't hurt us anymore. Whit said that when pilots were 'short' their duty changed to less dangerous missions. Everyone felt the intense pressure of surviving two more weeks, or one more week, or two more days. He was packing up all his gear now, getting ready to go and orienting his replacement, a new pilot fresh out of flight school from Beaufort, North Carolina. Just a year ago, Whit had been that pilot fresh out of flight school, landing in Saigon, hitching a ride up to Bien Hoa and walking head first into a war. Now, the new pilot taking his place would live in Whit's quarters and sit in that same chair writing letters home to his wife and family in Beaufort. She would read them, hoping and praying for his return, as we had for this long year, and I hoped that God would answer her prayers as He had mine.

In late November, as we were celebrating the idea of Whit's survival, the nation was still struggling under the weight of news about the latest combat, the limited success of the Paris peace talks and the presidential election that determined the new direction of the war in Vietnam. The political upheaval spilled out across our television screens and news commentators speculated about how each candidate might handle the conflict. "Conflict" was the word used now. No one shaping official policy wanted to call it war anymore. Politics became the thing that drove the fortunes of the war now, and we felt the emerging angst of our boys ending their short lives on a foreign battlefield to accommodate the political winds of government in an election year. The fortunes of the South Vietnamese people slid precariously away as each day of the war took them further from the victory that we all hoped for. They lived in the wreckage of a country now being slowly devoured by an insatiable enemy. What must their lives be like now. The ones who could escaped in small sampans drifting out into the South China Sea and picked up, thankfully, by our Navy ships. Others would follow and become the "boat people" who eventually found refuge in here America, starting over with families and friends who escaped the carnage and devastating loss of their country.

In the midst of our troubles we looked for hope, as we had over the long year of Whit's absence, and we found it in all the usual places. Myra called in fine spirits to say that she had a letter from Phil and he was coming home, the same time as Whit almost to the day. She planned to pick him up in New Orleans and come back to the apartment at the Bay Water. Then he wanted to go have Thanksgiving with his folks over in Columbus, Georgia. It looked like Phil and Whit both had orders to be stationed at Ft. Wyles again as instructors. She was torn between glad and sad. There was still so much to be sorted out between them. I wished she could be here with me to help plan Thanksgiving dinner. She claimed to be undomestic, but in reality, she had skills and made the best Coq Au Vin I ever ate. I made her recipe a few times, but it never tasted quite as good as hers. She thought I should just throw caution to the winds and make all of Whit's favorites. Cynthia and Ilene thought that was excessive, and a nice traditional dinner was what everyone wanted and expected. I never saw either one of them quite so excited, not even in the dressing room of Randolph's Department Store in Memphis.

We began the serious planning for Thanksgiving dinner with phone calls between Ilene and Cynthia and me debating what would and would not be on the menu. If Peach was here she would have had very definite opinions and cooked what ever she liked in her kitchen. We needed to remember that Christmas dinner had to be considered, too. We didn't want duplicates, so the peace talks of recipe diplomacy began and I became the recording secretary of the Thanksgiving Dinner Joint Task Force. I could tell that Whit was thrilled at the prospect of eating his first home cooked meal in a year. Life was beginning to be a thing not imagined for a long time…it was beginning to be fun. Turkey was a given, and dressing, mashed potatoes and gravy, our own corn and okra. Ilene wanted to do her creamed onions and a sweet potato casserole with all those little miniature marshmallows melted golden brown on top, and two pies, pecan (from our very own trees) and chocolate. Her chocolate pie had a full shot of Kentucky Straight Bourbon in it, topped with an obscene amount of whipped cream. Even that had bourbon in it, sprinkled with toasted pecans and shaved chocolate imported from a Chocolaterie in the small French village of Tain L'Hermitage. Ilene really liked her little treats. Cynthia would do the dressing because no ones was ever as good as hers, and shrimp cocktail because she knew some boat captain down in Biloxi who would deliver piles of them into her waiting hands right off the boat, or Whitney's hands anyway. And crab, she wanted crab, too, for that casserole dripping in butter and garlic that turned a man into putty, every time.

My own contributions would be the gigantic turkey ordered from Holland's Butcher Shop that would, hopefully, fit into

Peach's oven. I could do the mashed potatoes, the vegetables and a Hummingbird Cake, Whit's favorite. We decided to get three more large pies from Estelle; chess, pumpkin and lemon meringue. Cash was in charge of picking those up. And wine, Cynthia and I insisted on bottles of both red and white now that we were hardened wine drinkers. I was assigned the responsibility of going out in the dark of night to surreptitiously acquire nine bottles, three whites and three reds and three champagnes, from Eldridge's clandestine establishment. He had begun now to anticipate my purchases and always kept those bottles back for me, looking stoically away as he handed them over to me through his back window. I really wanted to wish him a Happy Thanksgiving, but he insisted on maintaining the bounds of decorum between us. Ilene firmly believed the men needed bourbon, the quiet libation associated with the gentle comforts of the porch, and the only acceptable elixir for easing the pain of consuming all that food, so I collected three bottles from the reserved stock in Eldridge's back room.

 The excitement of planning our dinner celebrating Whit's safe return grew beyond our immediate family, and in a bewildering chain of visits and phone calls, we found ourselves besieged with pleas from distant kin to be included. Were we really related to Martha Ann's mother's third cousin who was last seen alive helping roof the barn in the spring of 1953? Didn't we remember that Peach's older sister's husband's nephew had married one of the sisters who lived in the old Crenshaw house before her brother sold it to Dr. Walker's late mother-in-law, and then part of the roof collapsed from all that rain and she caught pneumonia? We had to draw the line somewhere, so it fell to Cynthia to manage the regrets, saying that later on, " We'll do an open house and have everybody in." She assumed command like a general, soothing the disappointed and marshaling us, her troops, reminding us to be nice to someone named Mrs. Wallace because we didn't want to have her feelings hurt. So, in my wanderings around town, I tried to be the soul of diplomacy. In the end we did have a completely full table of sixteen Blue Willow plates all squeezed in, plus more Blue Willow on card tables set up for Cash and Walter and the younger cousins they were supposed to ride herd on. We had to buy a whole extra ham and a tray of squash casserole from Sally's. Peach would have been proud.

Whit came back to us on November 20, 1968, landing from Oakland in the cold blue air of Memphis in the late afternoon. His journey began on one of the Freedom Birds, a 707 flying out of Da Nang bringing a planeload of our boys home. They even had two flight attendants, volunteers willing to brave the flights into and out of the hostile war zone. Whit said the plane was completely silent as they took off, as if everyone was holding their collective breath while they lifted slowly off the runway, climbing high into the sun and circling out toward the South China Sea. Then the voice of the pilot came over the intercom with an announcement.

— Ladies and gentlemen, we are now out of the airspace of South Vietnam.

A roar of cheers erupted, filling the cabin with the sound of men going home. The flight attendants had tears in their eyes. How often had they seen this moment, heard this roar of freedom, seen the relief on these young soldiers faces. Whit said he would never forget it. Later on, Charlie and Dave and Hardy all made it back to the states, home to the families that were waiting all these long days that make up a year of being away. Bradley got better and in the protracted months ahead, was discharged from the hospital in D. C. and wound up in the white house with the blue door on Cherry Street down from his parents in Tuscaloosa.

How desperate we all were for good news, how hungry for the things that really satisfied. It came to us in moments like these, in family dinners full of jovial conversation that disguised how deeply we desired the things that last. We all wanted different things and yet the same things. Whit was our lifeline, for Whitney and Cynthia, R. J. and Ilene and Isabel and me, Peach's "Sonny Boy." Now, he had come home to us and a million shattered pieces were suddenly mended. The fragile shells of our lives would survive unbroken. The thing we feared had not come upon us. Thanksgiving dinner was a blur of food piled high on Peach's Blue Willow dishes and conversation and celebration that left us all feeling an exhilaration we would never feel again in this life.

I imagined Peach with us, standing there, as she had done for years and years, reaching over to slice one of those pies. Her long buffet was buried underneath an embarrassing amount of pie and cake, a gentle reminder that there was plenty, more than plenty of everything we could have wanted in this life. We all understood it and felt it, the thing that finally allowed us to breath again. Every moment now was different, free from the gnawing fear that haunted our long specter of days. The thing we prayed for, hoped for, waited for had come to us. Whit was home and we all felt as if we would never again want anything as much as that. The relief set in the minute he walked through the door and set down his bags, looking just as he had when he left, only older now, and there was a weariness around his eyes that never went away. He had leave until after Christmas, when we would report to Ft.

Wyles over in south Alabama. But now, he had this blessed span of days to rest in his own bed beneath Peach's quilts and wander the tangled woods and watch the cows drift up from the golden fields at dusk and sit on the porch holding Isabel.

www.ingramcontent.com/pod-product-compliance
Lightning Source LLC
LaVergne TN
LVHW021235080526
838199LV00088B/4513